"Want to dance?"

A slow song played and the floor filled with couples. The lighting was low and thousands of white Christmas lights twinkled on the wood-beamed ceiling.

"Ah, sure." Garrett set his beer on the bar, then held out his hand to help her down. Eve's heels set her indecipherable stare at nearly his eye level, and wondering what was running through that pretty head of hers was making him nuts.

With his hands low on her hips and her cheek pressed to his chest, Garrett couldn't remember a time he'd been more confused. Holding her felt right. As if all that time between them had been erased and they were back in their high-school gym.

Could she feel the chaotic beat of his heart?

Eve looked up. Her eyes were shiny, but the hard set to her jaw said she wasn't about to let anything ruin their night.

He wanted to kiss her. Damn, he wanted to kiss her....

Dear Reader,

As I'm putting the final touches on Eve and Garrett's story, it's Mother's Day here in my "real" world. If you've read any of my previous books, you may have noticed I have an affection for children of all ages and when it comes to my own, I'm the world's biggest softy!

Because of my Mama Bear love for my brood, I struggled with the resolution to this story. While I won't give it away, it produced a surprising debate and made me really think about the way I might have handled the situation had it happened to me.

Especially on Mother's Day, I've always been happiest with my babies on my lap, but alas, they kind of grew up on me! My twins are twenty and my Russell will soon be twenty-one! When they were all little, I used to think those were the tough days, but now I know better. Diapers and late-night feedings have nothing on soothing broken hearts or proofing college papers.

My wish for all of you moms out there—and dads— is for you to always have your kids close, no matter their ages, if not physically, then at least in spirit. When it comes to love, as Eve and Garrett discover, no problem is insurmountable...just more of a challenge than they'd ever expected!

Happy reading!

Laura Marie

The SEAL's Stolen Child

LAURA MARIE ALTOM

HARLEQUIN®

entertain, enrich, inspire™

Recycling programs
for this product may
not exist in your area.

ISBN-13: 978-0-373-75434-2

THE SEAL'S STOLEN CHILD

Copyright © 2012 by Laura Marie Altom

ABOUT THE AUTHOR

After college (Go, Hogs!), bestselling, award-winning author Laura Marie Altom did a brief stint as an interior designer before becoming a stay-at-home mom to boy-girl twins and a bonus son. Always an avid romance reader, she knew it was time to try her hand at writing when she found herself replotting the afternoon soaps.

When not immersed in her next story, Laura teaches art at a local middle school. In her free time, she beats her kids at video games, tackles Mount Laundry and of course reads romance!

Laura loves hearing from readers at either P.O. Box 2074, Tulsa, OK 74101, or by email, BaliPalm@aol.com.

Love winning fun stuff? Check out www.lauramariealtom.com.

Books by Laura Marie Altom

HARLEQUIN AMERICAN ROMANCE

*U.S. Marshals
**Baby Boom
***The Buckhorn Ranch
‡Operation: Family

Competition for book dedications in this house is fierce, and this time, my not-so-little Terry won. He's had a rough year, but just finished a great semester at school and his father and I couldn't be more proud.

Love you, sweetie. I'm so excited to see what wonderful surprises your future holds.

Chapter One

"Garrett, thank you for coming." November rain fell in wind-driven sheets just beyond Barnesworth Mansion's two-story colonnade. Eve Barnesworth leaned against the imposing mahogany door, fingering her triple strand of pearls. "Calling this moment merely awkward would be the world's biggest understatement."

He cleared his throat, brushing past her with a nod. "That about sums it up."

"Can I take your coat?" Ever the perfect hostess, Eve held out her arms, glad to replace the inevitable hell to come with routine.

He shrugged off his rain-splattered pea jacket, handing it to her with a half smile. In the eight years since circumstance ripped them apart and she'd left their small Florida town, Garrett had changed from boy to man. He seemed taller. He'd become a navy SEAL, and the breadth of his chest and shoulders told the story of how physically powerful he'd become. His hair used to be on the long side when she could've spent hours fingering his curls. Now he wore it in a painfully neat regulation crew cut that struck her as distant and cold as his impenetrable gray eyes. In high school, she'd known every nuance and expression of his dear face. With time and tragedy between them—and more anger than she'd sometimes thought her heart could bear—she doubted she'd have even recognized him as her first love had they met in a crowd.

He cleared his throat, his gaze landing on the entry hall's chandelier. "You, ah, look well."

"Thank you." *But have you bothered to take one long look at me since you stepped in the door?* On such an upsetting occasion, it was understandable she'd be a well of emotions. Being on the verge of losing her father—her *everything*—was hard enough without tossing this reunion into the mix. Not sure what to do with her hands, she clasped them neatly against the small of her back. "Like I said on the phone, Daddy hasn't even told me what it is he has to say."

"Right." A nerve ticked on his hard, square jaw as Garrett nodded. "Well, I don't mean to rush something like this, but your dad and I have never exactly been close and with me only in town on holiday leave, we've got a houseful of folks at Mom's holding our Turkey Day dinner until I get home."

"Of course." Reading between the lines, Eve got the gist of Garrett's words. He didn't give a damn about her beloved father's deathbed request to see him any more than he'd cared to talk to her all those years ago. "I'll take you to Daddy's room."

TRAILING EVE UP AN ENDLESS flight of marble stairs, carefully avoiding the sight of her rounded derriere, Garrett Solomon might as well have been in the Buxton County courthouse for all the warmth this place contained. Because Eve's father, Hal, had been Coral Ridge's mayor

—like her grandfather—for the past forty years, it'd been dubbed the Mayoral Mansion.

Garrett preferred the Snob Hill nickname one of his football pals had thought up. Regardless of the name, the sentiment was the same—enter the old place at your own risk. Garrett might be a SEAL now, but back when he'd been sixteen, sneaking up the servants' staircase to Eve's room, he'd had no idea how many years of torment the occupants of this house would cause him.

"Just a little farther," Eve said, casting a half smile over her shoulder.

Right. The hall was wide enough to drive a VW Bug.

"Good. You're both here." Grim-faced Dr. Mulligan slapped his newspaper against the empty half of a brown leather settee. Garrett hadn't seen the man since he'd broken his arm at thirteen. "Hal's been calling for you, but gave me the boot."

"Sounds like Daddy…" Teary-eyed, Eve hugged the salt-and-pepper-haired doctor. "I—I can't thank you enough for being here. It's been a horrible few days."

"Agreed." The doctor stood, pulling open double doors that led into a dark room lit only by a bedside lamp. Antiseptic overrode the more putrid smells of sickness and pending death. Countless missions had taught Garrett that death indeed had a smell and it wasn't pretty.

A uniformed nurse sat near the patient, reading from the Bible. The old man had taken on religion a little late in life. "Mr. Barnesworth—" the woman moved to the foot of the bed, making room for Eve to stand near her father "—Eve is here."

"Garrett?" The old man's voice scratched as if he'd dined on sandpaper.

"I'm here." Though Garrett preferred the shadows, he stepped into the lamp's glow.

"Come closer," Hal said after a few shallow coughs.

"Daddy—" Eve perched on the side of his bed, taking his hand "—we can come back later if you're not feeling up for a talk."

"Nonsense." Waving toward the nurse and doctor, he managed through another round of coughs to dismiss them both. "Can't die in peace with this on my heart."

Garrett had been in a lot of strange places, but this one beat them all. The imposing, dark-paneled room housing a canopied bed suitable for royalty was about as welcoming as stepping into a museum exhibit. Not even the fire crackling in the hearth provided warmth.

"Go ahead, Daddy. Garrett and I are listening."

"We a-alone?"

His daughter nodded.

"Your baby—" Hal surrendered to another fit of coughs.

The old man's words tightened Garrett's chest.

If prideful Hal Barnesworth hadn't forced teenage Eve into some random, far-off home for unwed mothers, if Garrett had been allowed to care for her as he'd wanted, *their* baby might've lived.

"It's okay, Daddy. I forgive you for making me go."

With a violent shake of his head, the old man croaked, "No. N-not about that."

Garrett wasn't forgiving squat.

He might've been only seventeen when Hal told him his newborn son died, but that hadn't lessened the pain. Even years later, during mission com-blackouts, his mind couldn't resist playing a few rounds of what-ifs, plotting how different his life might be if not only his son had lived, but if Eve had cared enough about them both to stay in Coral Ridge.

"Y-your son," Hal whispered. "I'm sorry, but—" More coughs erupted.

Silent tears glistened on Eve's cheeks. Garrett knew the right thing would be going to her, offering her comfort during this obviously difficult time, but his feet felt frozen to the floor. Eve and her father once made his life a living hell. Could he now be blamed for not caring if the great Hal Barnesworth lived or died?

"Daddy, please." Eve gripped her father's gnarled hands. "Save your energy. Maybe if you rest, you'll feel better?"

After a particularly violent round of coughs, the already gaunt man seemed to shrink within himself. "Y-your son isn't d-d-dead."

"Shh…" Patting his hands, Eve said, "You're delusional. My baby died a long time ago. Like you said, it was for the best, right? His poor little heart couldn't support him. It was good he didn't suffer."

Really, Eve? You're drinking that Kool-Aid? How had losing their son been a good thing?

"I l-lied." More coughs.

"About what?" Interest finally piqued, Garrett moved closer to the bed.

"Your son's alive. I—I took him. I—" More coughs made his next few words inaudible, then he rasped, "My precious E-Eve…I'm sorry…I l-love…f-for best." He took a few deep, gasping breaths, then passed out.

"Daddy? Please, wake up. Tell me what you mean." Eve wrapped her arms around her father, hugging him to her. "Dr. Mulligan!"

The bedroom's doors burst open as the doctor hustled to the bed. "What happened?"

"One minute he was t-talking—" Eve wiped tears from her cheeks "—and then he—"

The doctor brushed her aside to check her father's vitals. "His blood pressure's dropped substantially in the past hour. Exhaustion's taking a toll."

"Do something!" Eve shrieked. "Call an ambulance."

"I'm sorry." The physician took a stethoscope from his suit coat pocket, gently nudging Eve aside. "Your dad signed a living will. With cancer and now pneumonia, he knew his time was coming and wished no extraordinary measures be taken to prolong the inevitable."

With Eve sobbing, hands over her face, and the doctor and nurse hovering over Hal, Garrett wasn't sure what to do. No doubt the old guy's words were just crazy ramblings. Also, knowing Hal, he'd no doubt wake in the morning—a good thing as he had major explaining to do.

Garrett knew he should be comforting Eve, but he couldn't bring himself to do it. He couldn't believe Hal Barnesworth might actually be dying, let alone that his confession may be true. Garrett's mind raced. His head knew this talk about their baby had to be just one more of Hal's manipulations, but why? What did he have to gain? If there was so much as a grain of truth to what the old man said, where was their son now?

Chills ran through him. So much emotion he feared he might be sick. Forcing himself to hold it together, Garrett drew on his training to force deep, calming breaths.

To the nurse, the doctor said in a hushed tone, "Please put ointment on Mr. Barnesworth's lips."

"Yes, Doctor."

Eve cried harder. "Ointment? Th-that's all you're going to do?"

The doctor ushered Eve into the hall.

Garrett followed, shutting the door behind him.

With his arm around Eve's slumped shoulders, the doctor said, "You have to understand, little things that help him be more comfortable are all your father *wants* us to do. Even if he didn't, drastic measures would only prolong the inevitable."

Begrudgingly, knowing it was the right thing, Garrett went to her, attempting a hug, only she pushed him away. "You hate him. Don't even try pretending you don't."

"Eve…" Not knowing what to do with his hands, Garrett crammed them into his pockets. "What I do or don't feel for your father has nothing to do with what we just heard. Think about it. I don't have a clue why, but your father has to be lying. You need to pull yourself together so when he wakes, we can drill him as to why he really wanted me here."

"I agree. What he said c-can't be true," she managed to cry between more sobs. "Daddy wouldn't do that to me. He wouldn't be that cruel."

"That's where you're wrong. You heard him—*for the best?* As in just like he controlled whether or not you were *allowed* to have a relationship with me. Seems your old man's playing games all over again."

"Stop!" Eve turned her back on him, but Garrett wasn't having it. She wasn't running from this, the way she had after their son's death.

"I, ah, need to make a call." Dr. Mulligan waved his phone before leaving the two of them alone.

"Look—" Garrett placed his hands on her shoulders and gently turned her to face him "—I'm sorry your dad's sick. I know you two are close. But if there's even the slightest chance what he said is true, we have to find out more. Hopefully, Hal's going to wake up. And when he does, we have to question him for definitive answers. We—"

"What's wrong with you? He's dying. But if there's any hope of him hanging on, I can't risk upsetting him again."

The doctor had returned and now paused alongside Garrett. "Maybe it's best you leave. I'm going to give Eve a sedative, and my nurse will stay with Hal through the night."

Tossing up his hands, Garrett laughed. "There we go with that word again—*best.* Oh, I'll leave for the night but, Eve, you've got exactly twelve hours until I'm back."

GARRETT'S FAMILY MAY have been waiting for him, but considering he'd just come out on the wrong end of playing emotional catch with a grenade, he wasn't ready to see them.

He'd have liked a hard run to work off the tension knotting his shoulders, but considering the Thanksgiving Day weather, he opted for the less healthy alternative of Schmitty's.

The bar and burger joint was good and dark. High wooden booths allowed for privacy. Loud '70s rock made it damn near impossible to think. When the waitress stopped by his table, he ordered a pitcher of beer.

But once she brought it, he was too shell-shocked to drink.

Hal's revelation had Garrett pissed. Actually he was beyond pissed. He had passed into some bizarre state he hadn't been in since he was seventeen and the old man told him his son had died. Logically, hearing the opposite should've sent his spirit soaring, but it wasn't that easy. On the off chance what the old man said had been true, even all-powerful Hal Barnesworth couldn't turn back time to rest that baby in Garrett's loving arms. And he would've loved his kid. Eve, too. They could've had it all, but their futures had been manipulated as though they'd been puppets on strings.

Their every choice had been stolen.

Worse yet, Eve seemed more concerned about her father's passing than the news that their son may actually be alive.

Chalk him up as a horrible person, but Garrett sure as hell wouldn't be sorry to see Hal Barnesworth go.

While all around him seeds of a good time were watered by beer and burgers into louder conversation and laughs, Garrett's mood grew proportionally darker. What if this was just the grand finale to Hal's puppet show? Garrett wouldn't put it past him to lie for the twisted amusement of seeing Eve and Garrett *dance*. But if Hal had spoken the truth? That meant somewhere out there Garrett and Eve had a son. Garrett's Thanksgiving leave was only a week, which didn't offer much time to find a child gone eight years. Even if Garrett eventually found him, what happened then? Was the kid happy and healthy? Assuming he was, then what? There wasn't exactly an *Idiot's Guide* written on how to tell an eight-year-old you were his dad.

Covering his face with his hands, Garrett struggled to find answers where there were none. He'd hoped to seek solace in the pitcher on the table, but had yet to take a drink. In order to process Hal's revelation he needed clarity, not a good buzz.

After thirty more minutes staring at the initials carved into the backrest of the wooden seat across from him, he finally paid his tab and exited the warm bar.

The night had grown even more ugly, wind driving rain so hard against his face that the drops nipped like teeth. In the car, he couldn't focus. Soaked, cold, his hands shook so bad it was a battle to work his Mustang's manual gearshift. While his mother lived only a few miles away at the foot of Coral Ridge's lone hill, the few-minutes' drive lasted a minilifetime.

Finally, he parked in front of the modest ranch-style home where his mom lived alone since his fireman father had died while on duty a few years back. Having nagged Garrett for grandchildren, what would she think of this possible twist of fate?

The Barnesworths were Florida royalty, local gods. After an obligatory round of questions ranging from what the house looked like to what designer Eve had been wearing, his mother finally got around to asking, "So? How was seeing Eve again? Is Hal as sick as she led you to believe?"

"Who knows?" Garrett shrugged off his coat, hanging it on a rack beside the door. "He's for sure bad off, but I wouldn't put it past him to rally, then live fifty more years just to torture me."

"Oh, dear…" Dina Solomon leaned forward from her seat on the couch. "What did he talk about?"

Garrett sighed, wishing for privacy instead of an

audience consisting of not only his mom, but maternal grandparents, his mom's sister Carol, brother-in-law Todd and their son, Zane. "I'm not sure I should say. Probably his big confession isn't even true."

"Now," Dina said, "you *have* to tell us." The group sat in the formal living room near the fire, being teased by the rich scent of Thanksgiving dinner still on hold in the kitchen. His mom usually went overboard when it came to decorating for holidays and this one was no exception. Life-size stuffed pilgrims stood smiling in a far corner, framed by dried cornstalks and, of course, a stuffed turkey.

"Bet the old man left Garrett a bundle," his twenty-year-old cousin Zane said.

"Put a sock in it." Garrett thumped the back of the kid's head. "Well, I can't believe it, but Eve and I might still share a connection."

Ashen, his mother—the only person present who'd known what he'd been through—frowned. "What's that mean? I thought this was the first time you've seen her since she left for—" she stopped herself from blurting where Eve had really gone "—finishing school?"

"It was."

"I went to an Easter egg hunt on the mansion grounds when I was a little girl." Grandma Fern sipped from her ever-present martini. The woman was already a touch senile. Why was his mom adding liquor to her already addled mind? "The gardens were like something from a fairy tale. Are they still as fancy?"

"I don't know, Grandma. It was dark and raining."

Dina adjusted the throw pillow nestled near the small of her mother's back. "I'm sure they're just as gorgeous as you remember." To Garrett, she said, "Go on, hon. What did Hal say?"

Tired of keeping everything secret, Garrett told them the whole story—including Hal summoning him to the mansion to inform him his son had been stillborn. Eve moved from the unwed mothers' home to an East Coast college prep school, then on to college. He hadn't spoken to her since she'd left town carrying his son. "Tonight, Hal coughed so hard he could hardly speak, but what he did manage to get out..." Garrett shook his head. "Hal said my son's alive."

Garrett's mom clutched the gold cross she always wore on a thin chain around her neck. "I have a grandson. Where is he? I want to see him now."

"Slow down." Garrett helped himself to someone's abandoned glass of white wine. "I'm having a hard time believing this is even true. If it is, our son may be out there, but Hal didn't say where. I'm going back in the morning. Hopefully, he'll tell us more. But my gut feeling is that it's a lie."

"Hal wouldn't lie on his deathbed. You'll find your son," Garrett's grandpa Ira assured him.

"Where's Eve now?" his mother asked.

"I assume with Hal. Best as I could, I tried comforting her, but she pushed me away."

"As much as we all want you here," his grandmother said, "you should go to her. I remember when her mother died like it was yesterday. Marianne Barnesworth was a lady through and through. Each public appearance, she and Eve were always matching, only Eve had that blond hair of hers fastened up in a big bow. When Marianne died in that car crash, the whole town nearly shut down. And the funeral—saddest thing ever.

Eve looked so small and alone. Those horrible photos of her standing graveside were published in most every paper in the state. Such a fragile little girl."

"Yeah—" Garrett shook his head "—well, now she's all grown-up and more than ever, wants nothing to do with me."

AT 1:57 FRIDAY MORNING, Eve's father died.

She refused the sedative the doctor had left and dismissed the nurse. What she needed was privacy—not coddling.

Hugging a bottle of merlot, grateful the staff and her father's longtime housekeeper, Juanita, were off with family for the holidays, she returned to her father's room. The coroner had taken her father's body a while ago and the nurse had changed the bed linens and removed all signs of this having been a makeshift hospital room. Even the sick scents had been sanitized away. Now all that remained of her once strong father was the faint trace of his spicy cologne.

Seated in a wing chair before the dancing fire, Eve poured the wine, but left her glass on the side table, too exhausted to lift it to her mouth.

Eyes closed, she struggled to wrap her mind around his words. *Your son isn't dead. I lied. For best.*

"Daddy," she whispered, "how could you?"

With her father's cancer, her divorce from Matthew only a year behind her, two miscarriages before that, she was afraid to hope she might truly have a son. For so long her mind had been focused on grief, she was afraid to even hope for light.

Lately, aside from work, it seemed her life had been nothing but a succession of grief-filled episodes. It'd been so long since she'd truly been happy, she feared permanently losing her smile.

But with this news...

She fumbled for her wineglass, taking a fortifying sip.

She'd loved Garrett more than she'd thought it possible to love. The only time she'd ever fought her father was when he'd sent her away. How different would her life be had she stayed? Faced the ridicule of her classmates and no doubt the whole town? How hard could it have been compared to losing Garrett? Their son?

My father. His admission compounded the pain of her most recent loss. Not only was he physically gone from her life, but she wasn't sure he was the man she'd forever admired. Forget the fact he was her dad—the one person she'd always believed unconditionally had her back. Where was his soul? Who told his own daughter her child died, then justified it by saying it was for the best? When was a lost child ever *best?*

Eve pressed the heels of her hands to her forehead and struggled to make sense out of a night that'd been sheer chaos.

Abandoning her wine, Eve sought her room—not the nondescript luxury guest room she'd slept in since leaving Matthew the year before, but the space she'd occupied in what felt like another life.

As dusty and disorganized as the place felt in her mind, it came as a shock to find it in pristine condition—as if none of the memorabilia, pictures and uniforms had actually been used, but were merely props for a catalog diorama.

Eve fingered her cheerleading skirt, recalling the thrill of working the crowd at her first varsity game.

Of Garrett kissing her after that game. He'd scored his first varsity-team touchdown and she'd rewarded him with what started out to be seven kisses, but ended as so much more. Her gaze skipped to history and chemistry texts that'd never been returned. To snapshots of her friends making faces in the locker room before that long-ago season's first basketball game. Garrett's Christmas gift—a giant stuffed alligator—still sporting his big, red bow. Folded love letters that'd been passed during class were in a box she'd decoupaged with magazine clippings she'd found in Coral Ridge High's blue-and-gold colors.

Having left school in January, she'd never gotten yearbooks for her junior and senior years, but as she perched on the foot of her bed, she flipped through page after page of sophomore memories, chest aching when tracing Garrett's image on the page they'd shared for being on the homecoming court. Funny how pics of her ex-husband, Matt, only made her angry. Seeing Garrett reminded her how rich and full her life at fifteen had been compared to now.

Two pages were dedicated to the class trip they'd taken to Disney World. Space Mountain had not only terrified her, but given her a wicked case of motion sickness. Garrett hadn't pressed her to get over it, like some of his jock friends. He'd bought her a Sprite with his precious lawn-mowing money, then held her hand while they'd explored what most of their crowd considered to be the more childish sections of the park. They'd ridden the boats on the "It's a Small World" ride five times, always laughing and singing along. That day, with Garrett by her side, she'd felt like the luckiest girl alive. Like nothing or no one would ever break them apart.

Throat aching for the many losses she'd suffered, she touched the tip of her finger to the phone number he'd childishly written on the photo sideways up his tie. They'd moved, necessitating the change to his home line. He'd wanted a cell, but his parents refused. How many times had she called? Lying on her pink striped comforter, talking with him until his mom yelled for him to go to bed.

Eyeing the phone on her nightstand, knowing Garrett's mom still lived in the same house, Eve couldn't help but wonder if the family number was also the same. If so, who would answer? Dina? What would she say? If Eve asked for Garrett, would his mother pass him the phone?

As badly as she'd earlier wished to be alone, she now craved her old boyfriend's company—not for any romantic sentiments—all of those were long gone. More to verify she hadn't been dreaming. That there really was a chance she might be a mother.

On autopilot, she lifted the handset. The low, flat dial tone seemed to fill the room, much the same as her pounding pulse reverberated in her ears.

Chapter Two

Garrett planned to be at Eve's by sunrise, but his mom talked him into the more reasonable hour of nine. A mistake. In the night, Hal had indeed died. The place now crawled with attorneys and funeral-home suits.

Upon ringing the front doorbell, he'd been greeted by a uniformed maid, then shown to the solarium. "Ms. Barnesworth will be with you shortly."

"Thanks."

This had been Eve's favorite room. Was it still?

Garrett had to admit, it was pretty cool. Outside, it was fifty and raining, yet in here the weather was always in the balmy eighties, smelling of loamy earth and sweet orchids. Beneath the domed glass ceiling resided a tropical rain forest, complete with palm trees, blooming hibiscus and a pair of huge, red lories. He couldn't believe the birds were still alive. What were their names? Rhett and Scarlett? Brick paths meandered alongside a slow-moving stream. In the massive room's center were wrought-iron tables surrounding a splashing, three-tiered fountain.

Garrett had a seat, trying to let the soothing surroundings calm his erratic thoughts. What if Hal's deathbed ramblings were true, and he and Eve did share a son? He was no P.I., and didn't have a clue how to find a child who no doubt Hal had wanted to remain lost.

"I almost called you." When Eve appeared, his pulse soared. She wore a figure-skimming black dress and matching pumps. Her long blond hair had been restrained in a fancy updo he didn't much like. This flawless woman wasn't the Eve his memory knew. He'd first loved her messy, wearing her red-and-white cheer warm-ups with a crooked ponytail, painting homecoming posters while sitting on the gym floor. A lousy painter, she'd always managed to get more on her and her surroundings than whatever she was supposed to be creating.

"Why didn't you?"

She shrugged, joining him at the table. "What would we have said? All of this seems easier handled in person."

"Probably true."

Hands clasped, she said, "Daddy's lawyer will be here soon. I find it easier to think out here than in my father's office."

"Agreed. Last time I was in there wasn't good."

"What did he say?"

Her question and overall fragility threw him off guard. How many times had he rehearsed what he'd do should their paths ever cross? Yet now, all of that escaped him. Her complexion pale, body rail thin, his sole thought was to wonder when she'd last had a decent meal.

Garrett cleared his throat. "Hal told me our baby died and that you'd chosen to complete your basic education in a Connecticut finishing school. Had Google been what it is now, I probably could've found you, but…" He shrugged. "Water under the bridge."

She stared past him, deep into her own world. "I was so devastated over losing the baby, I just did what I was told. To go from feeling life growing inside you, to grueling hours of lonesome labor, only to come out on the other side with my arms empty, I…"

"For what it's worth, I hurt, too. I used to have nightmares you'd died. I spent so much time moping my folks took me to a shrink. I know you loved your father, but I've gotta tell you, the man meant nothing but trouble to me."

"Good. You're both here." Barry Stevens had been Hal's personal attorney, friend and Coral Ridge bigwig for decades. Every edition of the *Coral Ridge Gazette* carried an ad for the guy's law firm featuring the Scales of Justice, along with Barry's meticulous swoop of white hair and supersize smile. Though they'd never formally met, the lawyer extended his hand and worked his trademark smile as if they were long-lost friends. "Garrett, good to see you. Each and every one of us here in town is darned proud of all you've accomplished."

"Thank you, sir." Garrett would've preferred a more flippant retort but, for Eve's sake, kept his sarcasm to himself. If he'd been president, it wouldn't have been good enough for Garrett to be with Hal's little girl.

"Okay." Barry set a few files on the table before taking his seat. "Eve has filled me in on her father's deathbed confession and in doing so, I believe, given me just cause to break attorney-client privilege."

"Wait…" The comprehension of this suit's admission hit Garrett harder than any stray bullet. So it was true? He actually had a son? Mind spinning, chest tight, he found it hard to breathe. During the endless night, he'd convinced himself the whole thing was a cruel joke. That in the morning, Hal would pop out of bed with his pompous barrel laugh, bragging about how he'd gotten them good. "You knew about this from day one, yet did nothing to stop it?"

"Slow down there, partner." Barry tidied his files. "My hands were tied."

Eve started to cry.

"The only thing Hal told me—and this was only after a couple glasses of Macallan Scotch—was that your son *hadn't* died. I pressed him for more, told him you both had a right to know, but he admitted neither of you had even wanted the baby, so this resolution was best. Absolved you both from any guilt, so you'd feel free to get on with your lives."

Barry reached out to comfort Eve, but she pushed him away. "Don't touch me."

The lawyer held up his hands. "I'm sorry. I advised Hal he'd handled the whole situation poorly, but he was insistent no one ever know."

"Where is our son now?" Garrett pressed clenched fists to his knees. There was so much he wanted—needed—to say, but what would going off on this guy solve?

"God's honest truth?" Barry's expression was sober. "I don't have a clue."

"How could he do this to me—us?" Seated in her father's oversize leather desk chair, Eve felt lost. Barry and his crew had long since left and she'd learned Hal had preplanned his funeral down to which hymns he wanted sung and what he wanted to wear. She'd known her father liked to be in charge, but one more revelation about just how controlling he truly had been might send her over the edge.

Garrett glanced up from the file he sifted through. "Wish there was something I could say or do. Pretty much from day one, I didn't hit it off with your old man, but I get how to you, he hung the moon. You've gotta feel like you're losing him twice."

"Yeah." It was uncanny how even after all the years between them, Garrett still knew her thoughts. Much more time together and they'd be back to finishing each other's sentences. "Find anything?"

He flashed her a half smile. "You own a cabin in Aspen."

"Swell." Covering her face with her hands, she sighed. "All this money, yet I'd trade every cent to turn back time."

"What would you do different?" He moved on to the next folder in a cabinet filled with hundreds—none labeled.

What a loaded question.

Would she go back far enough just to claim their baby? Or further still so that they'd never shared their first joke, kiss or attempt at making love?

"More like what wouldn't I do?" Cheeks superheated, she dived into her own file relating to the buying and selling of Exxon stock.

"You regret us ever being together?"

"I didn't say that." She moved on to the next file. "I just meant I've made a lot of mistakes."

"One of them being me?"

"Seriously?"

He shrugged. "I wasn't the one who for all practical purposes vanished. If you'd wanted, you could've found me a dozen different ways."

"It wasn't that easy," she lied. So what if she had called him or written? What good would it have done?

"My point, exactly. Because from my way of thinking, if you'd have told me where you were, I'd have done anything in my power to get you back. Hell, steal a car if I'd had to. That's how much you—" Suddenly he slapped his latest file to the finished stack and pushed himself up from the floor. "I've gotta get out of here. Clear my head."

"Garrett…"

The look he shot over his shoulder was painfully cold. "What?"

"Nothing." *Coward. Tell him how your dreams had been filled with just such scenarios. Of him riding to your rescue and the two of you, with your sweet baby, all living happily ever after.* "Are you coming back? We still have days' worth of paperwork to sift through."

"Yeah. I'm just going for a walk. Unlike you, I finish what I start."

GARRETT KNEW HIS WORDS were a low blow. Maybe even cruel, but Eve acted as if she wasn't even human. She might've shed a few polite tears over her father dying, but beyond that, she struck him as unflappable. Oh, her fragile appearance told him she possessed a full set of emotions, but she wasn't giving them away for the mere price of asking.

He'd loved her more than his own life.

Not only had he lost his son, but her.

Such plans he'd made for the three of them. He couldn't afford college—at least not right away, but their town had plenty of good factory jobs that would have allowed him to set them up in a starter apartment. Eve could've stayed home with the baby, or if she'd wanted, his mom probably would've watched their son to allow Eve to work at a part-time job. Sounded sappy, but while they might not have been living in a mansion, their little home would've been rich in love.

Gunmetal-gray sky threatened rain, and Garrett jogged back to Eve's. The sooner they found their son the better. If there was one thing this unexpected reunion had taught him, it was that his instinct to never trust the fairer sex—with the exception of his mom—was right on target. Eve's lack of communication hadn't just hurt him all those years ago, but annihilated his old way of life. He'd abandoned plans for finding a job, instead opting for the navy in the hopes hard work and a little adventure might raze the girl from his head. Only after entering the SEAL BUD/S training program had he been pushed to the point that he'd been physically incapable of thinking about Eve or their son. Only then had his healing begun.

What he'd never expected was that seeing her again would open old wounds.

Just as rain started to fall, Hal's housekeeper let him inside. Juanita had emigrated from Cuba and worked at the mansion for over twenty years. Round and perpetually smiling, she sported as many wigs as varieties of cookies he remembered her baking. Today, she'd gone for a full mane of red curls. "Miss Eve is napping, but she told me to tell you go in office and I bring you snack."

"Thanks, but I'm okay."

"Okay," she said with a firm nod and toss of her curls. "I bring sandwich."

Laughing, he knew no matter how much he'd learned during years of combat, when it came to battling Juanita, he'd never win. Which begged the question, how was Eve so dangerously thin?

After forcing down a hoagie, Garrett returned to work on Hal's files. How he'd run this town for so long when his own effects were in chaos was another mystery. He must've bought manila folders by the thousands, cramming them all into a few cabinets with seemingly no order. Stock certificates were housed alongside a newspaper clipping of Eve marching in a parade. If there was information to be gleaned in this office, it wasn't going to come easy.

"You're back." Eve still wore her dress and heels, but her once smooth hair was mussed. Had she actually succumbed to a nap?

"And?" She'd expected him to bolt.

"You're right, you know." Slipping off her heels, she curled onto the end of a leather sofa, drawing an afghan from the back to cover her legs. The night was cool enough to warrant a small fire in the hearth, which Garrett easily could've accomplished. Might be petty, but in their battle, he'd already given her too much ground. No way was he also volunteering to make her more comfortable. "I'll admit, back then, I owed you some sort of explanation—at the very least, a proper goodbye."

"I'm good. You don't owe me squat."

"Then why so bitter?" Her voice was soft, so soft. Just as he remembered, only throaty, sexy. Trouble was, she'd already destroyed him once and he damn sure wouldn't let her again.

"Why do you think? After eight years of mourning my son, I discover he's alive, only I don't have a clue where. My whole adult life I've trained to efficiently solve any problem, but this…" He shook his head. "We should hire a P.I."

"No. I'd like this handled as discreetly as possible. Losing my dad is painful enough. I don't want our search for our son to become a public spectacle. And for the record, you don't have to take your anger out on me. I'm just as much a victim as you. Daddy may have meant well, but that doesn't excuse him for committing a horrible wrong."

"True," he conceded. "But I'm not the one in my twenties, still calling a conniving old man *Daddy.* He committed a crime—against both of us. It doesn't matter whether he meant well or not. Had the man survived, I'd have had him charged with kidnapping."

"Please, Garrett," Eve quipped, "don't hold back. Let me know how you really feel."

"Geez, Mom." Garrett sat at the kitchen table and shoveled leftover turkey and gravy into his mouth. "I get that Eve loved Hal, but she seems to accept what her father did. Like she's resigned to the fact that what's done is done and there's nothing she can do about it."

Nursing her coffee, his mom asked, "You think she's wrong? That it will somehow serve her to hate the father she's only just lost?"

"What's the matter with you?" Eyes narrowed, Garrett dropped his fork to his plate. "Buying in to the whole Barnesworth small-town royalty facade?"

"Only because you're understandably on edge, I'm going to let that slide. I know next to nothing about Hal, but as your grandmother already told you, Eve's mother was an amazing woman. She did wonderful things for every charitable organization in town—nearly the whole state. All I'm saying is that I admire Eve for keeping her cool. In less than twenty-four hours, she's lost her father, gained a son and become the head of a miniempire that employs half this town."

Garrett helped himself to cranberry salad. "Thought old Hal was mayor."

"He was, but he also owned the canning and shoe factories, as well as at least a dozen other businesses all over Florida. Last I heard he has contracts with several big-name New York designers who want their brands made in the U.S.A."

Snorting, he said, "That supposed to make me feel better? That the lying old coot was at least patriotic? This is your grandson. Why aren't you more upset?"

"I am, but it's complicated." She rubbed the back of her neck before leaving him to refill her coffee. "When you told me and your dad Eve was pregnant, we were both so afraid for you. Had you two married, the odds against you would've been nearly insurmountable. Who knows? In a way, though it was unspeakably cruel, maybe Hal did do you two a favor. Can you honestly say you'd have made it through BUD/S with a newborn and wife?"

ON THE MORNING OF EVE'S father's funeral, the same church she'd been married in was now packed to standing room only. More people who'd come to show their respects lined the street outside. The same organist who'd played for the last Florida gubernatorial invocation hammered away on old Southern hymns. Considering her father had made all of his own plans, she'd have thought he'd hire a New Orleans jazz band. But then as much as he'd enjoyed a party, that would've been too much of a spectacle. He'd also enjoyed the nice, solemn ceremonies of life, so why wouldn't he also enjoy them in death?

As much as Eve longed to give in to the ball of emotions souring her stomach, she stayed strong as she knew her father would've wanted. Contrary to what Garrett believed, she refused to think her dad deliberately set out to hurt either of them.

The scents of roses, lilies, carnations and a dizzying assortment of other arranged flowers made her head pound and eyes water to such a degree she could hardly see the words on the hymnal's pages. It was only her allergies making her a wreck. No matter what, she refused to give in to her grief in this too public arena.

At the service's end, the funeral director whisked her into a white limo for the short trek to the cemetery where her father had wanted to be buried next to her mother in the family tomb.

Eyes stinging and throat hurting, she remembered sitting in the same spot over a decade earlier, only at least she'd had her father's hand to hold. Now she sat alone.

Though the day was sunny, a brisk, cold wind whipped the open tent sheltering the mourners. Tuning out the pastor's words, her mind's eye saw her father speaking what she now knew had been his last words.

I lied. Your son's alive. I took him.

She didn't want her thoughts to go there. Instead, she wanted to remember happy times. The two of them traveling to Europe together. Sharing morning tea in the solarium. She refused to think of him shrunken and sallow in his final days. He was the most powerful man she'd ever known and she'd been so proud to be his daughter. But now...

I lied.

Now a seed of doubt had been planted as to whether or not her father's motives had been pure.

Above all in life, evident by a funeral larger than any the town had ever seen, Hal Barnesworth valued his standing in the community. His reputation and pride. Had she returned home with a baby, his efforts to spirit her away to deliver her son far from his beloved town would've been for naught. Everyone would've known what an awful parent he'd been. After all, who didn't keep close enough watch on their teenage daughter and allowed her to end up pregnant?

He'd been ashamed of her and her actions and hid her away as surely as he would've a poor business decision.

Horrified by the emerging picture of who her father really was, she brought trembling hands to her mouth. When it came to his negative opinion of Hal, Garrett had been right. Was he here? Watching her? Thinking her a fool?

A gust of wind toppled the portrait of her father that he'd wanted displayed on a stand beside his casket. Though the funeral director leaped to action, promptly setting it back in place, Eve found the incident apropos. A symbol of how her mighty father had fallen—at least in her eyes.

Garrett, are you out there? Somewhere in the crowd? Did she want him to be?

Thankfully, the service soon ended and Eve went through the motions of placing a white rose the pastor handed her atop her father's casket, then thanking the crush of well-wishers for coming.

A Palm Beach caterer was setting up an invitation-only reception at the house, but all she wanted was to escape.

Voice hoarse from the sheer number of people she'd spoken with, she was unprepared when a stocky man approached, flashing her a *Miami Herald* press badge. "Eve Barnesworth?"

"Y-yes."

"I wonder if you might confirm a story I've got a lead on."

"Excuse me?"

"My source says your father employed a number of illegal immigrants, but bribed local officials to look the other way. Care to comment?"

Knees rubbery, Eve searched for something to steady her, but found only air. How could this day get worse? How insensitive was he to bring up such a hot-button topic here?

"Ma'am, a quote from you on this matter would be ideal, but this is going to make headline news regardless. Your father was a very well-known man."

"Please," she managed to whisper, world spinning. Unable to remember the last time she'd eaten, Eve struggled to stay on her feet. "Just go. I have nothing to say."

"Sure you do. Now that you're in charge of all Barnesworth holdings, you really gonna let *Daddy* get away with something like this when he repeatedly touted how his products help support the good ol' U.S.A.?"

"Please, would you—"

"Back off," Garrett said, suddenly at her side. She

leaned into him, beyond grateful for his strength when she had none.

"And if I choose not to?" the guy taunted.

Garrett made his decision for him—flattening him with one punch.

Chapter Three

"Do you have any idea how bad this makes our whole team look?"

Garrett winced, lowering his cell when his commanding officer, Mark Hewitt, grew so loud Garrett heard him just fine with the phone being nowhere near his ear.

"AP picked up the story—SEAL Slams Reporter at Funeral. It's everywhere."

"Sorry, but the guy had it coming." Whether his actions had been proper or not, Garrett figured the guy was lucky he'd gotten off with only one punch. Poor Eve had been a trembling, crying mess that Garrett had taken her straight home to his house—not hers. Hal's lawyer and Juanita were handling the reception. Dina had ordered Eve to the sofa, where she now slept.

"Agreed, but you know better."

"Sorry," Garrett repeated, hoping with enough contrition this would all go away. "What do you want me to do?"

Sighing, his CO said, "You're already on holiday leave for a few more days. Make it a few more weeks till this all dies down."

"You got it." Nice. Especially considering Garrett needed time to search for his son.

After five more minutes of hearing Mark lecture, Garrett finally was granted permission to end the call.

He found his mom out back, weeding. "Aren't you cold?"

"Nah." Kneeling in front of a baby banana palm, she rocked back on her heels. The wind had died down, though it was still chilly. When they'd moved to this house, he'd been midway through high school and had resented leaving the home where he'd grown up. Not only were there mature flower and vegetable gardens, but he and his dad had built a tree fort in their old yard that the kids living there today still enjoyed. Judging by how great this place now looked, his mom had put in a lot of gardening time. Back then, she'd told him the new yard would one day be beautiful, and as usual, she'd been right. "After all the rain we've had, feels good getting out of the house. How's Eve?"

"Sleeping. You think I was wrong for letting the reporter have it?"

"Honey…" She took a few beats to answer. "You know I'm not big on violence, but in this case…"

"My thoughts exactly." He sat on the wood bench his father's firehouse crew had presented them with. His dad used to spend hours out here. His family and his garden were the only things he'd put above his job. What would his pop have thought about all this? Telling his folks he'd gotten Eve pregnant had been one of the hardest things Garrett had ever had to do. They hadn't been overjoyed, but made it clear they'd stand by him no matter what. Given the chance, would he be that good of a dad?

"Say we find our son," Garrett said to Dina. "What then? I'm assuming he was adopted. If he's living in a good home, I can't see ripping him away from all he's ever known. But on the flip side, if we find he's not in an idyllic situation, then what?"

"Pace yourself, hon. Let's tackle one problem at a time."

EVE WOKE NOT sure where she was. Then she spotted Garrett lightly snoring in a recliner. A huge cat sprawled across his lap, purring so loud Eve heard him from across the room. Fat Albert was still alive? They'd found the Maine coon tail as a kitten under the football-stadium bleachers. She'd wanted to keep him, but her dad refused. Garrett's parents had recently lost their dachshund and were happy to take in the stray.

The whole Solomon house might've been small enough to fit in the ground floor of her home's east wing, but the decor's warmth made the space infinitely more inviting. The rooms were painted in soothing pale blues and yellows with most of the artwork either home-made needlework or paintings. Tables and shelves contained haphazard piles of books, and plants thrived on every windowsill.

Though Eve had missed her father's funeral reception, oddly enough, she wasn't sorry. Even if there hadn't been that scene with the reporter, she didn't feel emotionally strong enough to handle countless one-on-ones with family friends. As much as she valued their condolences, her father's deathbed revelations left her in an odd place. While she was mourning, she was also angered and saddened by her father's deception.

Toss in the possible illegal-immigrant scandal and it was too much.

Rising silently, she folded the quilt she'd been covered with, then went in search of Garrett's mom.

"Sleeping beauty!" Dina called from across the backyard. Neat weed piles told how she'd spent her afternoon. "Come look at these elephant ears. Last time you were here, I'd just planted them from bulbs."

Eve fought fresh tears. Her pregnancy and subsequent disappearance couldn't have hurt only Garrett. Understandably, Dina would also have been justified in being upset. How kind she was to not show it.

"They're lovely." Eve fingered the enormous leaves, breathing deeply of fresh-turned soil.

"Garrett still out?"

"Yes." The memory of him with his cat made Eve smile. "I can't believe you all still have Fat Albert—and he's bigger than ever."

"Us Solomons—" Dina tugged extra hard at a dandelion "—keep what's ours."

"If that was a dig about—"

"Stop right there. I may dig in my garden, but conversationally, I keep things on the up-and-up. If I have something to tell you, you'll know. All I meant was that whether it be a stray or the grandchild I've long dreamed of having—once you and Garrett bring him home—I'm going to hold on to my grandson for all I'm worth."

"Assuming we find him…" Garrett crossed the lawn. "You need to follow your own advice, Mom, and take this one step at a time."

Eve asked, "When do we stop talking about finding him and actually start our search?"

"SURE YOU'RE UP FOR THIS?" Garrett asked the next morning in Eve's entry hall as she gathered her purse and a light jacket. As usual, she looked dressed for a corporate board meeting in a cream-colored suit with her hair once again up. He was glad. It made her less approachable and therefore less appealing—at least that was the line he fed himself. She was still a beauty.

"I'm excited." She managed a forced smile. "But truthfully, also a little scared. I haven't been to that place since we lost our son."

"You'll be okay." Had they still been a couple, he'd have pulled her into a hug, or maybe just held her hand. Some small sign to show her he cared. The thing was, they weren't in any way connected other than by their shared past, which left him in an awkward spot.

"Here you yummy snacks." Juanita handed him a bulging paper bag. "Sandwich and cookies."

"Thanks." He accepted her gift and had no problem giving her an impromptu hug. Today's wig was straight, long and blond. Drawing back he winked. "You're looking good. It's a long drive to Savannah, and this will come in handy. Ready?" he asked Eve.

An hour later, silence had moved past awkward to just plain annoying.

On a bare stretch of interstate, he angled to face her. "Look, it's been a while since we've really talked. How about filling me in on what you've done for nearly the past decade."

She'd been staring out his Mustang's window, but now glanced his way. "College at Brown."

"Nice." He passed a slow pickup.

"Daddy—*Dad*—went there."

"Sorry about that dig. I get calling Hal *Daddy* is a Southern thing."

She'd retreated to focusing on the passing scenery. "I joined a sorority, but looking back on it, I'd have been better off on my own. I spent too much time wondering if all those girls somehow knew my dirty secret. Which in retrospect, I can thank my father for. Had he let me have our baby at home, sure, gossipy tongues would've wagged, but once the shock wore off, everyone would've accepted our child. It incenses me how many years I lost due to feeling like a second-class citizen. Like just because I'd gotten knocked-up in high school, I wasn't good enough to keep company with so-called 'nice girls.'"

"Don't hold back," Garrett teased.

"Sorry," she said with a shy smile, "but it actually felt good getting that out."

"Don't apologize to me. You're preaching to the choir on believing you should never have left Coral Ridge, and there sure as hell isn't a statute of limitations on hurt feelings or anger."

"True…" When she met his gaze, his stomach acted funny. Lord, but she was a fine-looking woman. Somehow she managed to pull off regal, cute and smoking hot all at the same time.

Attempting to get his mind off how awesome he used to feel kissing her, he said, "I remember Mom telling me you'd been married. Guess it was quite the social event in Coral Ridge."

Eve groaned. "Another mistake. Met Matthew my junior year. We shared some fun times. He was president of Dad's old fraternity and during a parent weekend, Matt earned Hal's seal of approval and that was that. We married right after graduation—of course Dad had the whole thing planned. Aside from picking my dress, pretty much everything else was set." Eve paused, looking slightly ashamed. "Is there anything in my life I haven't let my father do?"

Garrett fought the urge to clasp her hand. "I'm assuming your divorce was at least your idea?"

She laughed. "Daddy still has Matt on his Christmas-card list."

Dodging a fast-food bag that'd blown into his lane, Garrett mused, "At least you won't have to worry about that anymore."

"You're so not funny. Anyway, my degree is in marketing, so I'm part of that division in all Daddy's companies. I've already taken off a week. Makes me dizzy thinking how much there is to catch up on."

"With your dad out of the picture, are you now in charge?"

Her eyes teared. "I take it sensitivity training isn't a highlight of SEAL business?"

"What? I asked a valid question. Last thing I meant was to hurt you."

Reclining her seat, she curled onto her side, effectively hiding her face.

"I'm no expert, but isn't it customary for you to now ask about me?"

Using her jacket as a blanket, she did have one question. "Got anything I might use for a pillow?"

BEFORE GARRETT PICKED her up that morning, Eve had done an internet search for a church she remembered being near the home for unwed mothers she'd stayed at. Now that Garrett had found it, the task fell on her to find the three-story historic residence.

"I remember it being redbrick." She'd rolled down the tinted window for a better look. "It sat on two lots and there was a vegetable garden we all took turns tending. And a giant live oak. Unless the tree was harmed in a storm, it has to still be there."

He slowed for a stop sign. "Nothing on this street fits that description. Mark it off on your map and we'll go block by block till you see a place that looks familiar."

Six blocks later, they'd found what they were looking for—only the garden had been replaced by a parking lot and an ornate sign hung from a wrought-iron gate, announcing that the place was a B and B called The Live Oak Inn.

"Now what?" she asked Garrett. "What are we supposed to do when our first—and only—lead doesn't pan out?"

He pulled into the federal-style home's lot and parked. "We're not giving up that easy. Come on."

Ten minutes later, they shared a wicker table and iced teas with the home's owner on the back porch. The day was fine. Balmy with a playful breeze swaying ferns hanging from thin chains. A sweet, white flower Eve didn't recognize perfumed the air. Had it not been for the jet flying low en route to the airport, they might've been in an earlier century.

"When we bought the place five years ago," said Clara Duncan, middle-aged and sporting a Civil War–era costume complete with prim hair bun, "the house was in foreclosure. Because of that, our dealings were strictly with the bank. Miss Ginnie, our neighbor to the west, mentioned in passing this used to be a home for unwed mothers, but I'm sorry I don't know much more than that."

"It's okay." Eve traced the condensation on her slender glass. "We knew this was a long shot."

Garrett asked, "Is Miss Ginnie still around?"

"Of course. Would you like me to call her over?"

"That'd be great." Fresh hope raced Eve's pulse.

It didn't take long for Miss Ginnie to arrive, using a four-pronged cane to help navigate the porch stairs. "As I live and breathe." Through blue eyes not dulled by age, the older woman surveyed Eve who'd stood to introduce herself and shake the woman's hand. "You are about the right age to be one of Rose's girls."

Garrett had pulled out a chair for the elderly woman and, after more introductions, helped her sit down. Clara bustled off to get more tea and cookies.

Eve's mouth was so dry she doubted herself capable of swallowing a crumb.

"Thank you for coming," Garrett said, sharing the high points of their story. "Since Eve's father left no information regarding our son's current whereabouts—or even names of his adoptive parents—we're having to start with the basics in our search."

"I understand." When Clara returned with refreshments, Miss Ginnie helped herself to three sugar cookies. "I hate to be the bearer of bad news, but the reason this house was even sold is because Rose ran out of money. I would assume she kept records, but she had no family that I know of."

"Where is she now?" Garrett asked.

Miss Ginnie shrugged. "The only kin Rose claimed were her pregnant girls. Best she could, she tried making this home a happy place, but it was hard in the face of such pain. Teens aren't easy to deal with under normal circumstances. Toss hormones and Savannah heat into the mix and Lord have mercy were there some fireworks over here."

Eve remembered all too well. She hadn't been pampered like she'd been at home. She'd done her share of cooking and cleaning and even though as much as possible she'd kept to herself, some of the other girls had been cruel—taunting her about her lack of communication from her baby's father.

While Miss Ginnie rambled on about how some of the teens had come from less than desirable families, Eve caught herself studying Garrett. The way he seemed to exude tightly coiled physical power. As if at a moment's notice he'd be capable of leaping from his chair to tackle any contingent. The word *handsome* didn't do his angular face justice. Experience had taught her his gray eyes held the capacity to hurt or heal. There might now be crinkles at the corners from too much time in the sun, but essentially, on the outside, he was the same guy she'd fallen for all those years ago. How had he changed on the inside? How many times had she sat in this very spot, wondering what he was doing? Thinking? Had she been on his mind as often as he'd been on hers?

As if feeling her stare, he glanced her way. While Miss Ginnie rambled on, their eyes locked. Eve wanted to look down, but held her ground. Now wasn't the time to let on how scared she truly was—not just about the odds of them ever finding their son, but taking on her father's responsibilities and finding a way to cope with her growing fear that Hal hadn't been the person she'd thought he was. As for how she felt about her unexpected reunion with Garrett? She might never completely understand.

"Miss Ginnie, Clara—" Garrett rose. "While we can't thank you enough for talking with us, we don't have long to be in town and we still need to get to the Vital Records Office. Maybe someone there can help find Rose."

They said their goodbyes and then followed Clara's directions to reach the next stop on their journey, where they encountered a line leading out the door.

Already on edge, wrung out from the memories of her father essentially abandoning her with Miss Rose, Eve said, "This is probably a sign. We should just go."

"No way. We've come this far and need to see it through."

Exhaustion clung to her, making her limbs feel heavy and drugged.

"What's wrong?"

She shook her head, intending to keep her private issues inside, but then she found compassion in his eyes and he ever-so-lightly cupped his hands to her shoulders. The realization she was standing in an endless line in what might turn out to be an endless, fruitless search for their son... It was all too much—especially when what the two of them once shared was a dream. Like some far-off, hazy image of what she'd always dreamed her life could be. "I—I have to go."

"Where?" Still holding her, his gaze searched hers. "You're exactly where you need to be."

Was she? Before her father's cancer, she'd been a strong, self-supporting woman. She'd not only recognized she was miserable in a marriage that'd been lackluster from the start, but she'd taken on the business world and won. Landing contracts for the manufacturing of top New York fashion designers' shoes had been not only fiscally rewarding, but personally fulfilling. She'd finally felt as if she were coming into her own. As if she'd lived the past decade underwater and had only just been allowed air. Then Hal's cancer had struck hard and fast, and now she was constantly falling apart. She didn't recognize the woman fainting at funerals and skipping out on family obligations. For the sake of not only her sanity, but all of the people depending on her to run her father's companies, she had to pull herself together. Fast.

"Tell you what." Garrett fished in his jeans pocket, handing her his keys. "Go back to the car and nap or rock out to the radio or whatever you need to do. I'll handle this."

Lips pressed tight and fighting tears, she nodded, taking Garrett up on his offer.

IT TOOK AN HOUR FOR GARRETT to learn exactly nothing. Not only was there no birth certificate, but no record whatsoever of their baby even having been born—or having died.

More than anything, Garrett wanted to give in to the slow burning rage building inside. He'd honestly been dumb enough, naive enough, to believe even the all-powerful Hal Barnesworth wouldn't have been capable of pulling a stunt such as hiding his own grandson, but he'd been wrong.

In the crowded parking lot, Garrett found Eve asleep with the car's windows down. She looked at peace and he didn't want to ruin that.

He tried opening the driver's-side door quietly, but she bolted awake.

Some of her hair had spilled from her tight French twist, making her appear more like she had back in school. His fingers itched to reach out, sample the soft strands as he once had been free to do, but he instead kept his hands to himself and climbed behind the wheel.

What they'd once shared was as lost as their son.

"Well?" she asked, tidying her hair. "What'd you find out?"

Right hand fisted, he punched the steering wheel. "Not a damned thing."

Chapter Four

"Eve Barnesworth, you can just march those sweet buns of yours right back home."

"Thanks for the compliment, but you know what they say about there being no rest for the weary." Eve kept right on walking toward the elevator. Her assistant Darcie was not only a good friend, but held her MBA from the University of Florida, and in a pinch, could run Barnesworth Industries. There wasn't a day that passed when Eve wasn't appreciative to Human Resources for finding her. Following Eve into the car, Darcie pressed the button for the third floor.

"I thought the saying was 'no rest for the wicked'?"

Eve managed a smile. "That probably describes us, as well."

"True." Darcie may have only stood five feet tall, but she was a dynamo. Another reason Eve admired her was because she was a single mom. Back when she'd still believed her son had died at birth, Eve liked to think had he lived, she'd have been much like Darcie—scrapping her way to the top, no matter the odds stacked against her. Between her quick wit, adorable dimples and killer work ethic, it was all too tempting to hand Darcie the company reins while she in turn ran off to Fiji. "Sorry I missed Hal's funeral. Leo had a 103 fever and I couldn't leave him." Leo was Darcy's four-year-old son. Cute didn't begin describing his freckles, red curls and rotating assortment of missing teeth.

After Eve's last miscarriage, she'd secretly dreaded whenever Darcie brought her son to the office. The pain of losing yet another child had been too much to bear. Lately, Eve had been able to enjoy Leo, but now that she'd learned she may have her own son out there, she'd grown curious about what he might be like.

Eve gave her friend a squeeze. "I wouldn't have wanted you to leave the little guy—although I'm assuming you've heard Daddy's send-off wasn't exactly the dignified affair I'm sure he wanted?"

"Unfortunately, yes."

The cranky elevator finally dinged and Eve gestured for Darcie to lead the way onto their floor. Barnesworth Industries' official headquarters was located in the century-old former Buxton County hospital. What the place lacked in amenities, it made up for in charm. Cypress floors glowed and the pink, mission-style exterior had become a recognizable landmark to everyone within a hundred miles. Much of the building was rented out to other longtime partners, legal firms and coincidentally enough in light of the building's past, a few doctors. The Spanish-tiled lobby's vaulted ceiling and grand double staircase rivaled those of any historic hotel.

Well-wishes and hugs from most every employee she passed meant it took Eve another fifteen minutes to reach the corner office that had once been a patient dayroom. Tall windows welcomed in healing sun and Eve was determined to not let even the stack of ten newspapers that'd featured her father's funeral and the scandal bring her down.

"Sorry." Darcie dashed ahead to take away the pile of bad news. "Guess I should've asked Gladys to get those out of here, but I don't think she's coming in today. Zack was the one insisting, you know." Gladys was Hal's bosomy secretary. The woman was big as a house and bore the motto that if you got in her way, she'd mow you down like a wrecking ball. She'd been with Eve's dad from the start and had the loyalty and facial structure of a bulldog. What she lacked in physical beauty was more than made up for by the kind of inner beauty that seemed to get harder and harder to find. Zack, on the other hand, had been her father's right-hand man. A Harvard Law graduate, his fair hair and green gaze might've been easy on the eyes, but he was also beyond intimidating.

"It's all right." Eve winced. "I was kinda there when the story first broke." Finally seated in her comfy desk chair, she exhaled. She'd been working from home alongside her father for so long that a guilty part of her felt good to be back among the living. "Is Gladys all right?"

"She's had a tough time with Hal's death—we all have. Even though we knew it was coming, you know…"

"Sure." Eve ran her fingers over the desk's cool, wood surface, reminding herself this was what mattered. Her dad might be gone, but the business was still here, along with all the people whose livelihoods depended on her to keep the company running strong. Responsibility bore down on her shoulders, bringing on an instant headache and literal pain in her neck.

"I'll call her in a little bit. Tell her to take as much paid leave as she needs."

Eve's father had easily been one of the most recognizable figures in the state. Larger than life with a loud laugh and even louder temper. In his prime, the army veteran had been over six feet of muscle. In his older years, too much steak and heavy cream sauces had loaded on the pounds. He'd been generous with compliments and holiday bonuses, but those who crossed him learned to deeply regret it. Along with seemingly everyone else, Eve had once worshipped Hal. Now she wasn't sure what she felt for her father.

Darcie asked, "Want me to call her for you?"

"No." Eve powered up her computer. "She's practically family. I owe her a personal visit."

"That may well be." Darcie tugged at the curtains to keep sun from shining in Eve's eyes. "But you only lost your dad a few days ago. With all due respect, maybe you also need more time off?"

"Probably." Eve shook her head. "No, definitely, but part of the reason I came in today was to get my mind off of his dying. Right before he went, in true Hal Barnesworth style, he dropped a bombshell on me that still has my ears ringing."

"Oh?" Darcie dropped onto one of a pair of ivory leather guest chairs.

"Prepare to have your mind blown." By the time Eve relayed to her friend the events of the past couple days, Darcie's mouth hung open.

"I fail to see how even Hal could've pulled all of that off—especially without Zack knowing."

"That's just it. Daddy pulled this stunt long before Zack came on board. I'm sure not even Gladys knew."

Leaning forward, Darcie rested her elbows on Eve's desk. "While I'm still processing the fact that you have a mystery child, tell me more about Garrett. Is he handsome? You two have sparks? Was he excited by the prospect of you two sharing a son? Is he as larger-than-life as navy SEALs are made out to be, or is it all a bunch of hype?"

"If you ever pause for breath—" Eve cast a faint smile "—I'll fill you in. Plus, he's meeting me here in an hour, so if you're not stuck in a meeting, you can judge him for yourself."

GARRETT HAD DRIVEN BY what Coral Ridge residents dubbed the Pink Palace no doubt hundreds of times, yet he'd never stepped foot inside. Since he'd always considered Hal Barnesworth to be a bloated, power hungry, egotistical brute of a man, Garrett halfway expected Barnesworth corporate headquarters to feature a flame and pitchfork-themed decor, but upon stepping off the third-floor elevator, Garrett was welcomed into a serene office space buzzing with productivity and rich furnishings. Far from the theme featuring black-and-orange flames, monochromatic sand-colored everything save for the occasional potted palm and pricey-looking painting made him feel even further from his comfort zone than Barnesworth Mansion.

While waiting for Eve, a receptionist requested he park on a leather couch the color of his mother's Sunday pearls.

The formality only reinforced how different he and Eve truly were. They might share a son, but that was where all other comparisons ended. This kind of life wasn't for him. Like his father, Garrett needed plenty of fresh air and excitement.

That point noted, when Eve rounded a corner wearing creamy-colored slacks that made her legs go on for miles and an ultrafeminine, breast-hugging blouse with fabric looking too soft to be real, Garrett struggled for his next breath. Making matters worse, Eve sported a flawless side ponytail that all at once made her elegant, yet fun. Had her smile reached her eyes, he doubted he'd be capable of speech. Still no sleep? Even all her styling perfection couldn't hide her red, puffy gaze.

"Garrett." Rather than giving him the hug he stupidly craved, she extended her right hand. "Thanks for meeting me here. I needed to handle a few things."

"Sure." What did it mean that even after their simple handshake, he still felt her touch? "Need me to come back later?"

"No, not at all." She led him down a wide hall. "Since my mind is already occupied by our son, I'm happy for a break."

"Know the feeling." It came as a relief—knowing she was also consumed with finding their child.

Her private office was even more intimidating than the rest of the place. Walls lined with silver-framed photos of Eve smiling alongside faces he recognized from magazines and TV had him feeling all the more out of his league. When she sat at her desk, offering for him to take a guest chair, he had the oddest sensation of being in some swanky principal's office with her about to give him detention.

He took in the twelve-foot ceiling. "Quite a place you've got here…"

"It's okay. Daddy's decorator had more to do with it

than me. She wanted magazine coverage. All I wanted were plenty of windows and a comfy chair." She handed him a yellow legal pad on which she'd made notes. "I think our best course of action is trekking back to Savannah. Maybe through real-estate records, we can find a forwarding address for Rose."

"Worth a shot." He returned her paper. "But are you sure you're up for that? It's one thing discussing the woman who no doubt took our baby through a third party. Meeting her face-to-face may not be so easy."

"Let's face it, we could've just as easily run into her on our last trip. I had no idea the unwed mothers' home was closed." Her eyes welled, but she held her composure. "Rest assured, no matter the personal cost, I'll do whatever it takes to find our son."

GARRETT HAD LONG HEARD from his friends with small children how they were fast to fall asleep in the car. Eve apparently was no different. Thirty minutes into their return trip to Savannah, she lightly snored—a fact which, were she to discover, Garrett guessed she wouldn't like. Back in school, where her grades were concerned, she never settled for anything less than perfection. She'd made him feel like king of the world when she'd told him that's what the two of them together were—perfect.

How easy it would be—falling for her all over again. She might be a highly accomplished businesswoman, but she also carried an air of fragility that made him want to fight all her battles. His job was protecting those who couldn't protect themselves. Only what he felt for Eve was far from professional.

Ten minutes from their destination, he gave her a gentle nudge. "Wake up, sleepyhead."

"We're here already?" She lowered the visor to fuss with her hair. "I'm so sorry. I never meant to crash like that."

"It's okay. You're cute when you snore."

"I don't snore."

He laughed. Had he called it, or what?

"I don't."

"If you say so."

"Whatever." She folded her arms. "Are we almost there?"

"My GPS says ten minutes, but you know how that goes." In the past hour, the computer lady had advised him to take three alternate routes.

Though he wouldn't admit it to Eve, Garrett's stomach was uneasy. When they'd initially launched the search for their son, he'd assumed it would be no big deal. Now he fully grasped how difficult the task may prove to be. Not only logistically, but emotionally. They'd just gotten started and already he dreaded the letdown if today's search also left them empty-handed. Even worse was being with Eve. Just now, their banter had been fun, but he didn't need to flirt, he needed to find his son. Eve had destroyed him once, and no way was he opening himself up to that brand of pain again.

In just under nine minutes, they reached the Chatham County Courthouse.

Inside, Garrett noted one of the governmental departments they passed. "Good to know we can also get our mosquito problem handled while we're here."

Eve faintly smiled.

In the Tax Commissioner's Office, they researched

back taxes owed on Rose's former home, and after plenty of schmoozing over the baby pictures on the clerk's desk, Eve soon enough had Rose's current address.

During the twenty-mile drive to Lake Hudson, the mood was tense, which made Garrett nuts. Trying to lighten the vibe, he said, "You did good back there. I'm not sure we'd have gotten as much info as we did without your advanced people skills."

"I wasn't faking. Her baby boy really was adorable."

"I know, but— Never mind." Something about Eve's tone hit him wrong. He'd been trying to pay her a compliment, but she'd taken it the other way. Story of their short-lived relationship. Perfection, then too many miscommunications to count, then nothing at all. "You nervous about seeing Rose?"

"Yes."

"Care to elaborate?" Why was it so important for him to understand what she was feeling?

"Sorry..." Hands clasped on her lap, posture rigid, her former fragility had transformed to ice. As if she'd built a wall she had no intention of letting him breach. "Truth is, I'm not sure what I'm feeling. Part fear and resentment mixed with anticipation stemming from hoping she has answers." Though the teary smile she sent Garrett's way vanquished his irritation with her silence, part of him preferred he and Eve keep their distance. Seemed safer that way.

"HOW'RE YOU HOLDING UP?"

"So-so." Eve honestly wasn't sure. Standing on the front porch of a run-down house settled square in the center of a weed-choked lot filled Eve with not just dread, but sadness. Rose had been kind to her. It was hard seeing an elderly woman reduced to living this way. On the flip side, if Rose knowingly helped Eve's father deceive her, she deserved whatever fate deemed fit.

"Here goes nothing." Garrett knocked on the front door.

The sound startled a cat from an overturned plastic milk crate. Three kittens instantly mewed.

"Aw..." Eve knelt to pet the black-and-white furballs. "They're so tiny. Their eyes aren't even open." Rising with the kitten still in her arms, she glanced about the porch. "I don't see any food for the momma."

Garrett knocked again.

A white-haired woman wearing a housecoat and slippers stepped out onto the porch of the house next door. "If y'all are looking for Rose, she volunteers at the library. She'll probably be home in an hour."

"Thank you!" Eve waved.

"You're welcome!" Just as abruptly as the woman had emerged, she dashed back into her home.

"Wanna grab a bite to eat?" Garrett suggested. "That should take about an hour."

"Sure, but can we stop by a store?" The momma cat had returned, and now did figure eights around Eve's ankles. "We need cat food."

"Eve..." Garrett's look implied she was crazy, but Eve didn't care. Focusing on a creature alive and in need of help shifted her worry away from her all-consuming thoughts of her son.

"I have to do this, okay?"

"Sure." He met and held her gaze for an uncomfortably long time. Enough to leave her wondering what he thought of her. Was he as proud of her accomplishments as she was his? Did he find her as attractive as she did him? Was he equally as certain the effortless connection they'd once shared was forever lost? "Hop in the car and we'll find the nearest store."

"Thanks." For everything. Helping her escape from her own father's funeral to chauffeuring her on what may ultimately turn out to be a heartbreaking wild-goose chase.

"ONE THING I DON'T GET." Garrett nudged a fallen tree branch from the park trail on which they meandered after lunch. The small town only had two restaurants—one downtown diner and one truck stop out by the highway. Having opted for the bustling diner, he and Eve finished the pot-roast special ahead of schedule and still had time to kill. Suited Garrett just fine. The few minutes alone gave him the privacy he needed to get to the heart of a couple matters. "Your dad told us our son died for our benefit. But—no offense—Hal struck me as the kind of guy who never did anything for a purely altruistic motive."

"If you'd made that observation before his death, we'd have rumble. Now..." She sidestepped a puddle. "I'd have to agree. So if he didn't do it just to save his and my reputations, then why?"

The day was fine. Hard to believe Christmas was only a few weeks away considering the temperature was almost eighty. Still, the park they strolled through had already been decorated and giant foil candy canes lined the brick path. A three-man crew worked on assembling a small, fanciful house Garrett assumed was for Santa. In days, the place would be crawling with carolers and cocoa and funnel-cake vendors. What hurt most of all were the families he imagined. Fathers walking alongside their wives, kids riding high on shoulders. Big hands holding little sticky ones while waiting in line to see old Saint Nick.

Trying to shake off his funk, Garrett strove to change his focus, but that didn't help his mood, either.

The heat heightened Eve's long-familiar, often-dreamed-about scent. For her sixteenth birthday, Hal had ordered her a custom perfume made in Paris. She must still wear it. Lily of the valley blended with snapdragons and orange blossoms topped by a dash of sweet mystery he'd never been able to read. As if forgetting the time and circumstances between them, his pulse raced just being near her.

Garrett tried focusing on Hal's motives, but thoughts of anything other than his companion refused to come.

"Have any theories?" Eve asked. They'd reached the trail's end at the city square's far side.

"Truthfully—" he glanced at her "—I'd rather talk about us."

"O-okay." To say Eve was taken aback by Garrett's words would've been a major understatement.

A mom with a jogging stroller whizzed by. Her precious cargo was a chubby baby boy.

For Eve, the pain of not having her own child never stopped. After two miscarriages with Matt, she'd believed herself incapable of ever having a healthy child—until now. "Only I wasn't aware there was anything left to discuss." They'd reached a wooden bench. Knees strangely weak, she sat.

"You held all the power. At any time, you could've called me, but you didn't. Why?"

She closed her eyes, drinking in the sun's warmth. "It's complicated."

"My feeble, non-Barnesworth brain can handle it."

"I didn't mean it like that..." Intending to reassure him, she pressed her hand to his thigh, but then their old chemistry kicked in and when their eyes met, the simple comforting gesture felt somehow more. "The times were different. When Daddy sent me away, I was ashamed. I thought the whole world hated me—you included."

"But you were having my baby. How could I have done anything but love you?"

"I was sixteen. Alone in what was often a terrify-ing environment. I wasn't like the other girls. I'd never shared a room with four people, or a bathroom with twelve. I'd never cooked or cleaned or washed my own clothes. That place changed me, and—" Eyes stinging from the force of holding back tears, she pressed her hands over them. Damn Garrett for dredging all this up one second earlier than necessary. Most every night spent in that home for unwed mothers, she'd dreamed of him charging to her rescue, but by the harsh light of day, she'd realized the futility of those dreams. Had she returned to Coral Ridge, the scandal would've morti-fied her father. She'd have been embarrassed, too, by her own lack of judgment. Garrett had been poised to entertain offers for football scholarships. His family couldn't afford college. What if she had called him? Dragged him back into the mess that had become her life? She'd refused to stand in the way of his dreams.

"Another thing you've never told me... If your dad hadn't pulled this stunt, and you'd had a normal delivery, what then? Would you have called me? Or were you planning to give our child away? In which case, why does it even matter to you if our son lived or died?"

Chapter Five

It took every ounce of Eve's long-bred restraint not to slap Garrett for his question. Or maybe it was more guilt. Shame. Yes, the plan her dad had so carefully made for her had included giving the baby to a nice family who couldn't have one of their own, but the decision had always eaten her up inside. "O-on weekends, when Daddy came to visit, I'd mention thinking about you. How I thought you and I should talk about maybe keeping the baby. My father advised against it. Told me you'd moved on."

"And you believed him?" Garrett laughed, but the sound was hollow.

"Why wouldn't I?" She looked to her hands she held clenched on her lap. "Hal was my world."

"Funny." Garrett stood. "All this time, I thought your world had been me. You were sure as hell mine."

Silent tears streamed her cheeks. "What do you want from me?"

"I don't know." He approached her as if on the verge of wrapping her in a hug, but then stepped back. Hands in his jeans pockets, he said, "I begged my dad to ask one of his contacts at the police station to help find you—or at the very least, go with me to speak to your father. He refused. Said it wasn't his business. Him and my mom had some pretty big fights about how this was their grandchild, and wasn't my dad going to do anything about bringing him or her home." Turning introspective, he sighed. "My folks rarely fought, so when they did, I remember. I'll never forget my dad's voice during their worst battle—it was the most angry I've ever heard him, but he never got loud. If anything, he was spooky quiet. He grabbed my mom by her arm, practically dragging her into their room before closing the door. The only parts of their conversation I heard after that were 'drop it,' and 'you don't know what he's capable of.' I never put two and two together, but do you suppose Hal was the reason behind my dad refusing to help find you?"

"I don't know." Unsure what else to say, incensed by the question but mortified Garrett could be right, Eve turned toward the car. "We should get going. Rose is hopefully home by now."

"Sure." He took the keys from his pocket, then strode in the direction of his car.

Eve couldn't begin to catch up, but then maybe that was what he'd wanted. Looking back on it, it had been unconscionable to even consider giving their child up for adoption without asking Garrett's wishes, but nearly a decade earlier, times had been different—maybe not in big cities, but in Coral Ridge, tongues would still be wagging about an unwed sixteen-year-old mother.

Why do you care?

The question was innocuous enough, but it still stung. Hurting even worse was the fact that Eve honestly didn't know. At the time, her love for her father had outweighed all else—sadly, even Garrett.

"Rose Pincherre?" Garrett asked the frail woman who answered the sad little house's door. Eve stood behind him, brandishing cat food when what the woman really needed was a new roof and paint job.

"Yes." She peered around him to Eve. "Can I help you? Oh, my heavens..." Gnarled hands covering her mouth, the older woman shook her head. "Miss Eve Barnesworth. Is it really you?"

Eve lost it.

Considering their conversation in the park, the last thing Garrett wanted was to dole out sympathy to a woman who'd obviously had none for him, but his mother's training ran deep and no way was he just going to stand there watching her cry for a second time that day.

Garrett held her to him, giving her the privacy of hiding her face against his chest. That damned bag of cat food gouged his stomach, but he kept right on hugging her. Over her head, he introduced himself, then asked Rose, "We're here for information about what happened to our baby. Would it be all right if we come in?"

"By all means..." The woman stepped back, welcoming them into her home.

The house's surprisingly comfortable interior came as a shock, considering the abysmal exterior condition. Hardwood antique cabinets held pricey bric-a-brac, Tiffany lamps and leather-bound books. Victorian sofas upholstered in gold velvet were dotted with colorful fringed pillows. A calico cat lounged on a sunny windowsill, and a black cat napped in a yarn-filled basket. Garrett didn't find it all that strange that a woman of Rose's age would have nice, older furniture, but the supersize flat-screen TV hung over a marble fireplace combined with the latest-model iPad resting on a coffee table raised questions. Primarily, why the show of poverty on the outside, when inside, it seemed Rose Pincherre's home was nicely decked out? Why had she allowed her home in Savannah to enter into foreclosure? Had Rose won the lottery or a lawsuit? Or could there be a more sinister reason for her lavish lifestyle? Like she'd sold more than a few babies and had been smart enough to know when to say when. If that was the case, what superficial electronic toy had his son's sale price purchased?

The place didn't even smell like a typical old lady hermit's home. No medicinal scents of BENGAY or trace of cat pee or mold. Just lemony furniture polish and maybe a hint of fresh-baked gingersnaps.

"Pardon the mess." Rose bustled to tidy newspapers and fluff pillows. "Would either of you like tea? I have iced or hot."

"Hot tea would be lovely…" Trembling, Eve lowered herself onto the nearest settee.

"And you?" Rose hovered.

Garrett said, "Nothing, thank you."

Their hostess left them for the kitchen.

He sat beside Eve, wishing they were in a different place. Garrett wanted to put his arm around her, reassuring her everything would be okay, but nothing could be further from the truth. Instead of reaching to him for comfort, she hugged her bag of cat food.

With Rose out of the room, Garrett asked, "Find all of this odd?"

"What do you mean?" She sniffled.

"Look around. You insisted we stop off to buy cat food. Does that fatty in the windowsill look like he's starving?"

"Hush," Eve scolded. "This place is falling apart."

"On the outside. Take a good look in here."

She did. Dawning was slow to come, but it eventually showed in the form of widening eyes and her hands fluttering over her open mouth. "You don't think..."

"She sold all those babies?"

"Here we go." Rose set an heirloom silver tray loaded with an equally pricey tea set on the marble-topped coffee table. She flashed a bright smile. "I brought cookies, too. No one likes tea without a little something sweet." After filling a bone-china cup for Eve, she pinched a white cube with silver tongs. "Sugar?"

"N-no, thank you."

"I know better, but can never seem to get enough." Rose prepared her tea-filled, fine porcelain cup with four cubes before settling into the wing chair opposite them. "Now, what specifically would you like to know?"

Where to start? Garrett didn't want to spook her. On the other hand, he wanted the truth.

Clearing his throat, he said, "You may or may not have heard, but Eve's father, Hal Barnesworth, recently died."

"I read it in the paper. I'm so sorry, Eve. Your father was a wonderful man."

The cynic in Garrett couldn't help but wonder if the woman's positive view had been tainted by a large cash influx.

"Thank you," Eve managed to say.

"On his deathbed," Garrett said, "he admitted the son you told Eve had died is in fact alive. Mind telling us where he is?"

The color drained from Rose's face. The cookie she'd

half eaten fell from her fingers onto the floor. "I—I don't know what you're talking about."

"I trusted you." As if only just now remembering she was a strong, accomplished woman who was no longer Rose's helpless ward, Eve straightened her posture. "I trusted you, and you lied to my face. I went through hell, delivering our son. I heard him cry. And then he was whisked away. When I asked for him, you told me he died."

"He did." Standing, Rose went to the window, stroking her cat. The animal's purring and a ticking grandfather clock were the only sounds in the otherwise silent room. "Clearly, your father wasn't in his right mind. For you to show up after all this time, accusing me of such an unthinkable act—well…" Hands flighty, she paced, but then stilled as if regaining her composure. "You have to believe I would never be part of such a despicable act."

Eve stood and deposited the cat food alongside the tea set. "Give this to your cats. As for the line of bull you just fed us—save it."

"THAT COULD'VE GONE BETTER."

"If that's your stab at levity…" Eve directed the car's AC vent to blow on her flushed face. "I appreciate your effort, but honestly, I'm not sure I've ever been this upset. How can she live with herself? Lying to my face? *Our* faces?"

"Wish I had an answer for you." Making a left out of Rose's neighborhood, Garrett aimed his vehicle toward the main drag leading to the highway. "More than that, I wish we had a way to prove she lied. With your dad dead, it's our word against hers."

She angled to face him. "What about Daddy's lawyer? What if we sic him on her?"

"Worth a try. But with Barry having no more documentation than we do, my gut feeling is we're back to square one. Again."

"MISS EVE—" JUANITA FOLLOWED Eve up the front staircase and into her room—the guest room—not the place where she'd spent her childhood, where painful memories resided. Even on her occasional trips home from college, and later with Matt, she'd always opted for the guest room. Her old room had become a time capsule. The neatnik in her knew she should carefully pack away those mementos along with their memories, but to do so would mean immersing herself for hours in a previous life she struggled to forget. It was far easier to shut the door. Only visiting when she was feeling brave. "You must come down to eat dinner."

"Thank you," Eve said from the top of the stairs, as she removed her too-tall pumps, "but I'm not hungry."

"You eat!" The woman who had been a second mom to her stayed close on Eve's heels. Many nights the two of them shared dinner, then watched TV or played board games while her father had been off at some party or dinner. "You too skinny. How you get Mr. Garrett love you if you no meat on bones?" Wagging her finger, she added, "Men no like scrawny chicken."

"Thank you for the advice." On her closet's threshold, Eve gave Juanita a hug. For the first time in, she couldn't remember when, Juanita wasn't wearing a wig. Her natural hair was long, dark and pretty with a hint of gray. On occasion, during late-night treks to the kitchen, Eve had caught glimpses of Juanita sitting at the vanity in her room, brushing one hundred strokes, counting aloud in Spanish. Tonight, she wore her hair slicked back in a neat, highly uncharacteristic bun. "But it's not like that with Garrett and me."

"Pssh." With a dismissive wave of her hands, Juanita said, "You not know what you talk about. Let me fix you nice, hot bath. Then you feel pretty and call Mr. Garrett. I cook for him, too."

"Juanita, please…" Too late. The matchmaker was already in the bathroom with the water running.

Eve removed her pearls, setting them on the crystal tray engraved with her initials that her father had given her as an engagement gift when she told him she'd accepted Matt's proposal. As Matt had already asked Hal's permission, her father had the gift waiting. The tray also held an assortment of rings, earrings and a tennis bracelet and matching necklace. Eve used to look at the tray each night when removing her day's jewelry and smile. She'd think fondly of her father's many gifts and of all the years he'd been by her side, protecting her, watching over her in every way a father should.

But now all of that had changed.

She wasn't sure what to think. Had any part of their relationship not been a lie? Had all this jewelry she'd thought given from his heart truly been means for him to alleviate guilt? Would he really have stooped so low as to have even somehow influenced Garrett's dad?

And then there was Garrett himself. In the short while they'd searched for their son, he'd been a rock. Why hadn't she gone to him all those years ago? He'd deserved that—to be part of the decision regarding their coming child.

Everything about the man was attractive—far beyond his physical attributes. It didn't matter that when he'd held her on Rose's porch her pulse had run away. What mattered was that after the disaster she and Matt had made of their lives, when it came to romance, Eve was done.

Matt had cheated on her—multiple times. But oddly enough, it hadn't been that that killed their marriage, but more Eve's own issues.

After two miscarriages, her failed marriage didn't even come as a surprise, but more a foregone conclusion.

"Water ready, Miss Eve." Juanita beamed. "You take nice, long soak, then I bring you dinner in bed and you watch funny shows on the television. Mr. Garrett he watch, too."

Bless her heart. Juanita wanted only the best for Eve—a grown woman she still viewed as her little-girl charge. But how did Eve politely make her understand no amount of bubble baths or butter and gravy-laden comfort meals or even Garrett's surprisingly good company would fix the gnawing ache in her heart?

Regret consumed her. Sorrow for the way she'd destroyed the magic she and Garrett once shared. She should've called him from Rose's. Later from prep school. Later still from college.

But what could she have possibly said to make up for how much pain she'd already caused? Not only had she left him, but back then, she'd believed herself responsible for the death of their son.

"THANK YOU FOR AGREEING to meet here." When Eve stood behind her office desk, extending her hand for Garrett to shake, he fought an irrational pang of annoy-

ance. They'd already been through so much. The fact
that she saw him only worthy of a handshake put him on
edge. But then realistically, what did he want from her?
Despite their current shared quest, they were virtual
strangers. He hadn't seen her in well over eight years.
"I've had all of Dad's files couriered over. Thought it
might be more comfortable having an actual table to
work on, rather than his office floor."

"Agreed." Her smile unraveled him. He saw past her
all-business, polished exterior to the free spirit she'd
once been. He saw her cheering him from the sidelines at his football games, her hair swept into a high,
messy ponytail, her smile urging him to a greatness
he'd never wanted more. In her, he'd found all things
possible. No dream too big. No matter how much he
knew a reunion with her would only inevitably lead to
more pain, he craved that young woman he'd fallen for
all those years ago.

Hours passed during which little conversation combined with zero clues as to where Hal might've hidden
their son only raised Garrett's level of frustration.

Slapping his latest dead-end lead alongside the sandwich he'd ordered for lunch hours ago, Garrett sighed.
"Riddle me this—if your dad sold our son, seems like
he'd have kept some financial trail. I mean, we've found
receipts dating back to the seventies for shoes. Only
makes sense he'd have somehow documented a trans-
action involving the sale of his own grandchild."

"You're right." Pushing aside the chicken-salad
sandwich she'd barely taken two bites of, she covered
her face with her hands. Outside, the gloomy day had
faded to night. Rain pelted the windows. The air drifting through the few that were open smelled heavy and

dank. How many times on nights just like this had he held her on the overstuffed sofa in the mansion's movie room? "But on the flip side, what if you're not? What if Daddy just gave our child away?"

"That'd be risky, too." A bread crumb clung to her lower lip. What was wrong with him that when he should've been solely focused on the task at hand, he was consumed by wondering if kissing that crumb away would be half as satisfying as he imagined? Striving to get back on track, he said, "If he did give our son away, it would have to have been to someone he knew well. Do you have any family members who may not have been able to have children of their own?"

Hands to her forehead, she groaned. "None that jump out, but I like where you're going with this. If there's one thing this search has taught me, it's that Daddy wasn't the paragon of perfection I believed him to be. This illegal-immigrant issue brought to my attention at his funeral of all places has become a logistical nightmare. Many of those workers are good people. Instead of helping them forge documents, why couldn't he have put our resources behind obtaining legitimate documentation?"

"More questions." Garrett bit into his sandwich. "I'm sick of them."

"Want to get out of here? Grab a drink?"

"Whoa…" Cracking a half smile, Garrett couldn't resist teasing, "I wasn't aware perfect princesses ever imbibed—let alone with the likes of me."

Her glare wasn't entirely devoid of warmth. "Before you read too much into my offer, my only other option is returning home to Juanita, who's on a mission to fatten me up and marry me off."

Gathering his trash, Garrett asked, "Who's the lucky groom?"

"You."

He coughed on the last swig of his Coke. "And here I thought Juanita and I had a thing."

"If you don't mind my asking—" she gathered her coat and hit the switch on the office lights "—why hasn't some girl snagged you a long time ago?"

"*Snagged* me?" Trailing behind her toward the elevator, enjoying the view of her well-rounded derriere in a hip-hugging black skirt, Garrett couldn't help but laugh. Her legs went on for miles and her heels only increased his pent-up physical frustration. Damn, she was sexy. "I haven't been caught, because I don't want to be. You taught me early on women are fun in small doses, but that's as close as I care to be."

"Any day now, you can quit blaming me for what happened, Garrett." She pressed the elevator's down button.

"I never blamed you for getting pregnant." He followed her into the elevator car, punching the lobby *L.* "Silent Night" played over the intercom speaker. It was annoying as hell. Reminded him Christmas was only weeks away and he was as far from feeling in the holiday spirit as it was possible to get. "If anything, I was secretly psyched. You having my baby meant we pretty much had to get married. We'd get a small house and buy our own dishes and silverware and stuff. We might not have been able to afford a TV, but we could've lounged on a lumpy mattress, staring at your tummy to watch the baby kick. I loved you, Eve. You meant everything to me."

"We were kids." With the elevator still not moving,

she punched the *L* button again and again. "You weren't even smart enough to realize on our own with a baby that world of yours would've eaten us alive. I mean, so far your fantasy has us in a house with a lumpy mattress, dishes and silverware, but no food. You couldn't even get a factory job without your high-school diploma, but how would you have finished school, working full-time to support me?" The car finally lurched downward. "I'm sorry, but you've spun this fantasy for us that never stood a chance of surviving."

Why did she do it? Just when he thought they might have the slimmest chance at reconnecting, she blew it all to hell.

Chapter Six

"Good, you're home."

Garrett entered his mom's home to find her struggling to assemble her fake Christmas tree. Back when his dad had been alive, they'd always had a live tree. Now she was on a save-the-world kick and believed her efforts in rescuing one fir tree would make all the difference. "Silent Night" still dogged him, only this time in a reggae version playing on the stereo.

"I can't carry the ladder in by myself and I baked two new cookie recipes I need you to sample before I take them to my bridge-night cookie swap."

Garrett fell into his dad's old recliner with a groan.

"You're tired. I'll bring you the cookies, then, once you're rested, you can get the ladder."

Why hadn't he gone for a drink with Eve?

Oh, yeah, because she'd royally ticked him off.

Pushing up from the comfortable chair he'd planned on spending his night in, he felt more mentally drained and bone-weary exhausted than he had after any SEAL mission.

In the kitchen, he pulled out a stool at the counter. "I want to run something past you."

"Shoot." She set a cookie plate in front of him, then hit the fridge for milk.

"Last night, I told you my suspicions that Rose was a professional baby trader. But today, Eve and I tossed around a new theory that had nothing to do with Rose. What if old Hal really did have a heart and instead of selling our baby, he gave him away? Do you remember anyone in town suddenly appearing with an infant around that time?"

Nibbling a frosted stocking-shaped cookie, she took a second to think about it. "No one immediately comes to mind. But the Barnesworths ran in a different social circle. Have you tried looking at local birth announcements posted around the time your son would've been born? It's a long shot, but you never know."

"Good thinking. We'll go that route tomorrow." He pointed to the toffee-oatmeal cookies he'd sampled. "I like this one."

Nose wrinkled, she said, "It's not very festive."

He waved off her concern. "They taste amazing. No need for anything fancy."

"Speaking of fancy…" She finished loading a plastic snowman tray with cookies, wrapping it in red cellophane. "How has it been working with the always-elegant Eve?"

Where did he start? Frustrating. Exhilarating. Confusing as hell. Garrett's mind told him he'd already blown it once with the woman. Last thing he needed was getting messed up with her again. His SEAL friend Deacon was one of the lucky ones who'd managed to merge a happy home life with their often ridiculously demanding job. The few times Garrett had even tried getting serious with a woman, either she'd nagged him endlessly about not having enough time for her, or cheated on him. In the end, it was easier being alone.

"That good being back with her, huh?"

"Sorry…" Garrett shook his head. "Got lost in thought. Eve is proving impossible to read." Making matters worse was the fact that the more time Garrett spent with her, the more he craved. He knew that was stupid, but what was he supposed to do about it? He sure couldn't hash it out with his mom.

"She's been through so much." Dina took a fresh batch of oatmeal cookies from the oven. The spicy, cinnamon scent made his stomach growl. "Give her more time, and I'm sure she'll come around. You two will be right back where you used to be."

"You think that's such a wise idea? Hooking up all over again? We live in separate worlds."

She winked. "Unless your next mission is to Mars, your worlds are fine. Your individual stubborn streaks are another story…." She winked again. "Invite the poor girl over for caroling. She'll get a kick out of it."

He snorted. "Right. More likely, she'll kick me."

"THIS WAS A GREAT IDEA." Eve was trying hard to cover the awkwardness she felt from practically sitting on Garrett's lap. They searched the *Coral Ridge Gazette's* ancient microfiche system that'd been set up in a lonely corner of a warehouse holding back editions. The space was so narrow, two chairs barely fit, and with Eve's thigh pressed against Garrett's—not to mention her shoulder and forearm brushing his—concentrating was growing tougher by the minute. "I'm sure anyone who welcomed a new baby into their home would be excited and want to publicly share their blessing."

"Unless they were also scared to be found out. I can see no questions being asked back in, say, the twenties, but, Eve, this isn't *that* long ago."

"But how do you hide a baby? You'd have to get a birth certificate, social-security card and immunizations. I suppose you could put off all of that until school, but eventually—unless these people are hiding our child in their basement—they had to have welcomed him in society in some way."

He stared at her, cocking his head before taking something from her hair. Brandishing a dust bunny, he said, "Once we get out of here, figured this might tarnish your perfect image."

Head bowed, she asked, "Is that how you think of me? As an unapproachable ice queen?"

"More like an unapproachable ice princess," he admitted with a half laugh. "You have to be at least fifty to be a queen. And anyway, do you even own a pair of sweats or a T-shirt?"

"Okay, first, that was a mean thing to say. Second, of course I own lots of stupid T-shirts." Only she didn't make a habit of wearing them in front of people unless she felt comfortable. She used to feel that way about Garrett. With her dad out of town and Juanita busy cooking dinner, they used to lounge in her room, wearing nothing but their birthday suits. The memory of his bare skin brushing hers made her cheeks glow. She tried scooting her chair away, but had no luck.

"Sorry. But seriously, when's the last time you wore a T-shirt?"

"Give it a rest." They'd both leaned in toward the screen. His radiant heat had nothing on the sweet scent of the lemonade they'd had for lunch still flavoring his breath. *If I kissed you, would you kiss me back?* Argh. What was wrong with her? Clearly, all this heat she couldn't escape and most especially her racing pulse were signs she was coming down with a nasty bug. "We still have at least twenty editions to go through."

"Just answer me. If I bought you a T-shirt, would you wear it?"

"Why does it matter?" She turned the microfiche reader to the next page. "You're acting crazy."

"More like bored. My gut feeling is this is a dead end."

Facing him, she asked, "Then why are we here?"

"Got any better ideas for what we should be doing?"

Heat again rose in her cheeks. Why did her mind keep running to the gutter? Why was she suddenly consumed with thoughts of what they might be like together again now that they both knew what they were doing? Back in high school, they'd been each other's firsts. Laughing through those awkward initial attempts at what eventually came more naturally than breathing. They'd slipped off to a secret garden on the grounds of the Barnesworth estate. There, they'd been all alone and beauty reigned. Beauty of innocence lost and rediscovered. Beauty of first love. Beauty of exploration and learning each other's every nuance. Of the few lovers Eve had had—including her ex-husband—Garrett had been the best. Or was that just her memory putting him on a pedestal where he had no right to be?

"We could divide and conquer," he suggested, already out of his chair. "I'll head to the courthouse and check out birth certificates."

Nodding, she struggled to focus on the screen in front of her, rather than sneaking a peak at Garrett's strong profile. At only three in the afternoon, he sported whisker growth. He was all rugged man—such an oddity in her social circle. Just one more reason why the two of them as a couple would never work.

With him no longer beside her, unexpected loneliness set in.

From the door, he asked, "Want to meet up later to compare notes?"

"Sure." But only if she squelched the giddy excitement that usually stemmed from seeing him again. "Name the time and place."

"I can always use a good burger. How about Schmitty's? Say seven?"

"Perfect." Though she'd never even considered going to the dive bar way on the wrong side of town, she wouldn't tell him that. Truthfully, she hadn't had many burgers, either. But just one wouldn't kill her.

Sitting next to Garrett, on the other hand? That just might.

"You're taking this way too seriously." Fluffing her red curls in Eve's bedroom vanity mirror, Darcie blew kisses at her reflection. Her mom had taken Leo for the night and in a little over an hour, she had a hot date with Chad from Accounting.

From her closet, Eve shouted, "He called me an unapproachable ice princess! Damn him, I'm a nice person!" Eve shouldn't have cared what Garrett thought of her, but his assessment stung—more so since her ex had pretty much said the same.

"Honey, no one said you're not nice." Darcie now tried on diamond and pearl bracelets. "Just sometimes you can be stiff. You know, formal—like you're not really one of us little people."

"Of course I am." She held out an emerald-green Gucci asymmetrical jersey dress. "How about this? The bare shoulder screams fun."

Darcie rolled her eyes. "If you're attending a garden party with the governor."

"If you're so smart about fashion—" Eve gestured her into the closet "—then you figure out what I'm sup- posed to wear."

Twenty minutes later, Darcie sat on the tufted bench in the shoe area's center. "I thought you were lying, but you truly don't own a pair of jeans—and your velour sweats don't count."

"So what am I supposed to do? I pride myself on knowing just what to wear to any occasion, but this..." Joining her friend on the bench, Eve rested her elbows on her knees and chin in her hands.

"Perhaps the more important question is why you care. I thought you and Garrett as a couple were *waaay* in the past?"

"We are." Fingering her pearls, Eve wasn't sure how to explain why this night with Garrett meant so much. In part, because she didn't understand herself. These past few days with him had shown a chink in her armor she hadn't even been aware had been missing—how much she craved the simple pleasure of being around someone to lean on. Sure, in a pinch, Darcie or Juanita were always there, but something about the way Garrett had held her at Rose's struck an old familiar chord. "It's just that he's been great through this search. I wouldn't blame him if he was furious with me, but he's been re- markably kind." Eve's pulse raced remembering him literally carrying her from that awful scene at her father's funeral. The way he'd driven in circles through Rose's town to find a grocery for Eve to buy cat food. When it'd been apparent Rose's outward show of poverty was a front, he hadn't even put in a dig by commenting how mushy she'd been in the face of possibly starving kittens.

She was now head of a miniempire. Time to man up.

But how was she supposed to do that when the more time spent with Garrett reminded her just how little she'd ever wanted her current life? Back in high school, she'd never dreamed of becoming a businesswoman. Sure, she'd wanted some kind of career—but something fun. Maybe in fashion design.

Mostly what she'd doodled on her spiral notebooks was the phrase "Mrs. Eve Solomon." What she'd fallen asleep dreaming of at night were images of the perfect family they'd one day have. Garrett would be a fireman like his dad and she'd help lots of charities like her mom.

"Ask me—" Darcie tried on the lace, peep-toe Louboutin heels Eve had worn to New York Fashion Week "—you've never gotten over this guy."

"That's crazy talk." Tapping her watch, Eve said, "Focus. I've only got a couple hours till meeting Garrett and I don't want to look like an idiot. I don't want to stand out in a crowd, but actually belong."

"But, sweetie—" Darcie smoothed Eve's hair "—what makes you think you don't belong? Everyone loves you."

"Do they?" Gripping her friend's hands, Eve blurted, "Is it really me they love, or the fact that I was Hal Barnesworth's daughter? Since Daddy died, I feel adrift. He was my anchor—only he wasn't the great man I'd built him up to be. If he was such a mess, what does that say about me? About every decision I've ever made?" *Especially all those years ago when I cut ties with Garrett.*

"Now you're the one talking crazy..." Wiping tears from Eve's cheeks, Darcie said, "Come on, let's take you shopping. Everything else will work itself out in time."

"Damn..." Garrett stood from his stool at the bar. Though Schmitty's was still hopping from the after-work crowd, all male eyes—especially his—focused on Eve. What had she done? Long legs hugged by faded denim topped by a skintight red T sporting a mistletoe sprig. Written in script across breasts straining the thin fabric was You Know What to Do.... Her hair was long and straight and makeup bold. Full lips holly berry–red. He'd been fiercely attracted to her as a teen, but now that she was all woman—whew. Even her sky-high red heels were sexy. Despite his vow to never lose his head over a woman again, he discreetly shifted his fly. "You look amazing. What's the occasion?"

After stealing his breath with her smile, she took the stool next to his. "We're having burgers. And you did give me an awful lot of grief over not owning a T-shirt. Had to prove you wrong."

He appraised the sensational full length of her. "And *that* just happened to be in your closet?"

"Does it matter? I'm starving."

Laughing, he handed her one of the laminated single-page menus. "I'm having beer. Want one?"

"Why not."

"Indeed."

Flirty country songs played on the jukebox and by

the time they'd each downed two beers and succulent burgers accompanied by the best fries in the state, Garrett felt nice and loose. After the tension of the past few days, the sensation—even if temporary—of being worry free was good.

"So tell me—" he tipped back his third longneck "—what's got into you tonight? Here we are, supposed to be all business—comparing our search notes—but if I didn't know better, I'd think I was dining with your bad-girl twin."

Picking at the foil label on her nearest empty bottle, she shrugged. "Guess your needling about that stupid T-shirt got to me. Had a minimeltdown after that and voilà—here I am. The new and improved, hopefully less uptight, Eve Barnesworth."

"I liked the old one just fine." He gave her hand a nudge—though he was damned if he didn't crave more. Like escorting her out onto the dance floor and holding her close even on fast songs. She brought out a fierce protective streak in him. For all her money and now power, she'd always struck him as a lost little girl in need of saving. Too bad when she'd needed him most, she'd pushed him away.

"Thanks, but if there's one thing this search for our son has taught me, it's that I should've stuck up for myself a long time ago when it came to my dad's edicts."

"You mean about me?" Easy enough for her to say she'd wished she'd contacted him, but that wasn't going to make the fact that she hadn't even bothered to call Garrett magically go away.

"You. Our son. Other things." She sighed. "Since Daddy's passing, I feel like I'm only just now seeing things clearly. Like up until now, my whole life was

viewed first through his filter— Trust me, I know
this must sound like a cop-out, but I genuinely want
to change. I want Barnesworth businesses to be run
with the beyond-reproach integrity they were when my
grandfather was at the helm. I want to find our son."
She bowed her head. "Most of all, I want to make things
right with you."

Mouth dry, Garrett wasn't sure what to say. What did
she even mean? Did she want things back the way they'd
once been between them? Or for them to be friends? Her
statement was as cryptic as the odd-shaped box *Santa*
had left under his tree for Christmas. Not to mention,
infinitely more intriguing.

"Wanna dance?" A slow song played and the floor
had filled with couples. The lighting was low and thousands of white Christmas lights twinkled on the wood-
beamed ceiling.

"Ah, sure." He set his beer on the bar, then held out
his hand to help her down. Her heels had her indecipherable stare at nearly his eye level, and wondering what was running through that pretty head of hers
made him nuts.

With his hands low on her hips and her cheek pressed
to his chest, Garrett couldn't remember a time he'd been
more confused. Holding her felt right. As if all that time
between them had been erased and they were back in
their high-school gym.

Could she feel the chaotic beat of his heart?

She looked up. Her eyes were shiny, as if tears were
pending, but the hard set to her jaw said she wasn't
about to let anything ruin their night.

He wanted to kiss her. Damn, he wanted to kiss her.
Need for her tugged him in a hundred directions. If he

followed base urges, then what? They'd already tried a relationship and it hadn't worked.

But then she took his every fear and replaced them with pure pleasure. She kissed him slow and hard and with just enough pressure to let him know she'd been craving him, too.

Through song after song, they danced and made out like teens, and didn't talk—in fact, made it a point not to talk. In the morning, none of this might even turn out to be real, but for now, he wanted all of her more than he could bear.

"Wanna get out of here?" he asked in a low tone, almost afraid of her answer.

Hands pressed to his chest, she nodded. "Where?"

"It's not fancy, but there's a perfectly good motel down the street."

"Yes."

"Sure?"

She answered with a kiss.

Chapter Seven

What are you doing?

Finally alone in the room Garrett had paid for with cash, Eve lightly shivered. The night had been balmy when she'd entered the bar—far too warm for a coat. Now the air had turned chilly—at least until Garrett ran his hands up her arms to warm her, sending his heat shimmering through her.

"You're so beautiful…" He cupped her cheek and she leaned into his touch. "I've wanted this for so long it feels like a dream."

"I know." She slipped her hands under his T-shirt, exploring the impossibly toned ripples of his abs. He'd been in good shape in high school, but now, his physical perfection was daunting. What would he think of her?

When she next kissed him, she worked his button-fly jeans undone. His arousal was no secret and when she cupped him, he groaned with pleasure.

He peeled her T-shirt over her head, tossing it onto a dresser, then lowered his attentions to her breasts, suckling hard through her scrap of a bra. Swelling and achy with need, she pressed him closer, running her fingers along his soft hair.

He paused to jerk the spread and blanket from the

bed, then snagged her around her waist, tugging her on top of him. Her hair veiled his face, but he framed her cheeks, kissing her, kissing her, sweeping her tongue. He tasted of beer and smelled of his hauntingly familiar masculine blend of sun and sweat.

While the rational part of her told her to stop this before it got further out of hand, truthfully, that was exactly what she wanted. More than anything, she wanted to feel whole again—like a strong, capable woman who wasn't all the time crying, but fighting for what she wanted. At the moment, Garrett very much fit that bill.

"Take this off." She yanked at his shirt.

"Yes, ma'am." Light from the parking lot illuminated his broad shoulders and rock-solid chest. He was a professional warrior and one hundred percent looked the part.

She wriggled free of her jeans, then helped him with his.

"What's got into you?" he asked, slowing her down. "We've got all night."

Not really. At any moment, she might lose her nerve.

"I want you now." *Need you.*

"I don't have protection."

"It's okay." Remembering the trouble he used to have with her bras, she removed it for him.

"Eve…" Still in his boxers, Garrett rolled onto his side, resting his head on his fist. "What are you doing?"

"I don't know what you mean." Was she not good enough for him? Had she hurt him so badly he was no longer interested? "Would you just hurry up and do this?"

"Whoa." Hands high in surrender, he sat up. "Now I know something's messing with your head."

"Don't you find me attractive?" Her throat knotted.

He sighed. "Not to be crass, but the size of my erection doesn't lie. Make no mistake, I want you as bad as I've ever wanted any woman, but not like this. Not with you acting as if a personal demon's nipping your heels."

"You're wrong." On his side of the bed, she straddled him, kissing him quiet and then blazing a moist trail down his chest and lower until the last thing on his mind was more talking.

With her on top, she took him into her. At first, his size was painful—it'd been so long, but then her body adjusted to welcome him in. With each stroke, she alternately blossomed and wilted. Being with him now brought pure joy. Knowing this must never happen again brought unspeakable pain.

Tonight, she'd given herself a free pass to be whoever she wanted. In the morning, however, she had to revert to old ways. She had literally thousands of employees depending on her to keep a clear head. Beyond that, Garrett deserved more. A whole and complete woman who could one day give him the children he deserved and who'd raise them as well as his mother had him.

Over and over she struck a rhythm old as time.

He pressed his hands to her hips, rising to meet her.

Sooner than she'd have liked, the sweet pressure building and spreading inside her shimmered in blinding white. Garrett tensed and the feel of his spilling seed only served as a lonely reminder that inside her, his child would never again find a home.

FAR TOO SOBER, GARRETT bunched pillows beneath his head and stared at the ceiling while Eve showered. She'd been consenting—hell, she'd practically thrown herself at him, so why, when they should've been cuddling, breaking down all that had gone wrong between them, was he on his own, feeling helpless while listening to her sob?

Finally having had enough, he went to her, drawing back the curtain to find her shivering beneath the water's cold spray, hugging her knees.

"Eve…" After turning off the water, he grabbed an armful of towels. Climbing into the tub, he sat behind her, tenderly wrapping her, holding her until her shivers and tears subsided. "When you're ready, tell me what this was about."

"L-love to," she said through a sniffle, "once I figure it out myself."

"You haven't grieved your dad. Think you're missing him?"

She half laughed. "What's funny—I don't miss him as much as the man I thought he was. The warm, funny, caring father I centered my life around was a lie, and I'm scared I'm only on the verge of those lies unraveling."

Stroking Eve's hair, Garrett listened, tried understanding how she'd seen such a different image of Hal than he had. For Garrett, Hal represented the locked gate that'd led to Eve. Eve—all he'd ever wanted. Yet now, all they'd once shared seemed dreamlike. As with dreams, they were fleeting. Once gone, they didn't come back. Garrett loved this woman more than he'd imagined it possible to love. Now? He feared never again feeling that deeply. In the same breath, he was scared of once again hurting that deeply.

The two of them hadn't made love tonight; they'd had sex. And it was great. But it didn't change the truth between them—that there wasn't a *them*. Would never be. Couldn't be. And that made Garrett sad, but more determined than ever to see this search for their son through. While the two of them as a couple may not work out, maybe—just maybe—finding their son would.

"You gonna be okay?" He kissed the top of her head. The tenderness he felt for her stemmed from somewhere deep inside he didn't wholly understand. In this moment, he recognized that despite their physical separation, because of their shared past, she'd forever be a part of him.

She nodded. "I needed to break down to be able to get back up."

"I get that." He kissed her again. Not as a lover, but as a dear, long-lost friend. "Thank you for feeling safe enough to be able to show your truth to me. I won't—could never—judge you."

"Thank you for that." When she snuggled against him, her warmth and trust swelled his chest. Carried him to a good place he feared he'd never be again.

THE NEXT AFTERNOON DARCIE winced upon hearing Eve's retelling of her night with Garrett. Eve almost wished she hadn't told her. "When we got you all dolled up to have fun, I never thought you two would end up in bed."

"Me, neither." Perched on the corner of Darcie's desk, Eve sighed. "The worst thing is, after my meltdown, he held me, and no matter how hard I tried convincing myself that wasn't what I wanted—you know, being close to him on that kind of level—it felt so good, that physical closeness." She covered her face with her hands. "What a mess. I can't be into him. And even if he was interested in me, what would I offer? When it comes to relationships, I'm a broken shell. First, I allowed my dad to call my every move, then Matt, then my dad again. I have to figure out how to care for myself before even thinking of taking on someone else. Beyond that, we share this lost son—a son I'm responsible for losing. Why didn't I ask more questions? At the very least ask to see his little body? What was wrong with me that I just let my dad handle the whole situation? Especially dismissing Garrett as if he were no more important than a gardener."

"Sweetie, you were only sixteen." Her friend gave Eve a hug. "Nobody makes all the right decisions at any age—let alone as a teenager."

Eve shook her head. "I'm not using age as an excuse."

"So what? You planning on living the rest of your life blaming yourself for a tough situation your dad essentially stole from your control?"

"I don't know what to do. And now there's the whole illegal-immigrant mess to deal with here. I spent the morning fielding questions from reporters. They seem to think my trying to now help make those employees legal is a smoke screen for some nefarious bigger plan. Like because it's the Christmas season, I'm trying to spin the negative publicity. It's nuts. Really, deeply nuts."

Taking two Snickers bars from her bottom drawer, Darcie offered one to Eve, then leaned back in her chair to unwrap her treat. "How about we tackle one issue at a time? First, we stress eat with a little chocolate, then everything else will seem better."

Eve raised her candy in a toast. "From your lips to God's ears."

"LOOK, LET'S GO AHEAD and get this elephant out in the open." Garrett set the file he'd been reading on the conference table in the room next to Eve's office. They'd set up shop there for the night, continuing what was starting to feel like a never-ending search through Hal's mountain of files. Outside holiday lights seemed to immerse the entire town in a happy glow, but between the two of them gloom ruled. "We had sex. It was great, but that was last night and tonight, we need to get through as many of these files as possible. Preferably while being able to speak to each other in a civil manner at least."

Ducking behind an open file, Eve said, "I'm not the slightest bit upset."

"Then what's with your deep freeze? We live in Florida and it was a pretty fabulous day. So why am I now cold as hell?"

At that, she laughed. "I'm embarrassed, okay? The woman I was last night…"

Garrett leaned across the table to lower the file. Her beauty never failed to take his breath away and this time was no exception. Eyes clear, makeup fading to make way for her natural glow, her hair long and a little messier than she probably liked… The mere sight of her made his heart skip a beat. "The woman you were last night was a wildcat." He kissed the tip of her nose. "And I liked her. And I liked her even more when she showed herself to be a real live, vulnerable human just like the rest of us."

Heat rose in her cheeks. "We should get back to work."

"Should we?" He took her file and closed it. "As much as I want to find our son, tonight, I think there's something more important we should do."

Eyes wide, she shook her head. "Oh, no, not another trip to Schmitty's."

"Get your mind out of the gutter." Holding out his hand to her, he said, "We're going to do something we haven't done since you dragged me along with freshman choir."

"Christmas caroling?" Eyebrows raised, she noted, "You hated to sing."

"Still do. But I also hate disappointing my mom and she asked us to go."

"I don't know..." Worrying her lower lip, she wrinkled her nose. "I'm assuming this is with her church crowd? What if we don't fit in?"

He squeezed her hand. "What if we don't worry about anything other than grabbing our fair share of hot cocoa and Santa cookies waiting for us back at Mom's house when we're done?"

"DASHING THROUGH THE SNOW..." Eve hadn't realized how much she'd missed the simple act of singing. By the time she and Garrett and his mom's Bible-study group had belted out tunes at ten houses, her throat was already tired—but in a good way.

"Having fun?" Garrett nudged her side as they trudged down Baker Street toward their next audience.

"Yeah, I am. After Mom died, Daddy was never big on Christmas. Juanita always puts up decorations, but that was more out of formality and expectations than because of his overflowing holiday spirit."

"What about the crafty stuff we made in elementary school? He never displayed it?" In addition to sharing their first two years of high school, they'd also shared junior high and second through fifth grade. "Mom still puts up cinnamon-stick reindeer and those god-awful ugly green paper plates with our crooked pictures on them."

The new knot in Eve's throat had nothing to do with too much singing. "Not sure what happened to all of my stuff. Maybe we'll find it in one of Daddy's files."

"Sorry." When Garrett took her hand, Eve didn't fight him. They'd hung at the back of the crowd and under the cloak of night, none of his mother's group could see them. Simple human contact felt as good as singing. Not that their brief sexual encounter hadn't been amazing, but Garrett holding her afterward had been even better. The air smelled sweet, of winter-blooming flowers and humidity rolling in from the Gulf. "I know so many kids who were jealous of you back in school, but even though you had a brand-new Mercedes and all the latest clothes, you missed out on a lot."

"Thanks for reminding me." She released his hand, only to have him snatch hers back.

"I wasn't trying to hurt your feelings. Just never occurred to me you had troubles, too. You might not've had to slave away your weekends working at Burger Barn, but you had your own issues to deal with."

"I guess." Eve had never thought of her younger years that way, but looking back on them, having to always be perfectly behaved had been difficult. In a sense, when Eve's father had paraded her out at dinner parties, having made sure Juanita dressed her in fancy gowns matching the color of his ties, she'd been a quasi stand-in for her mother. Not a woman, but not a child.

Changing the subject, she asked, "What's your gut feeling on the kind of childhood our son is having?"

"Part of me thinks if Hal was brazen enough to sell

him, it would've been to a family who could afford to buy a child—not that having money qualifies anyone to necessarily be an expert parent." He released her hand to shove his in his jeans pocket.

"If that was a dig at my dad, I'm sure he did the best with me as he knew how. Before Mom's accident, when I wasn't in school or art or ballet, I spent most of my free time with her. When she died, he was as lost as me. Maybe even more so because he'd been forced to become my mother and father." Without Garrett's hold, Eve now felt cool despite the night's balmy temperature. What chilled her more was that no matter how much she stood up for her father, the fact remained that he had committed a monstrous, unconscionable act. And she wasn't sure how she'd ever forgive him.

The group arrived in front of a ranch house decorated in blinking blue lights. Though Eve had been very much enjoying the night, when a family came out the front door to listen and applaud, the sight of three small children dressed in footie pajamas, framed by clearly adoring parents, tore at Eve's heart. How would her life have been different had her mother lived? An even more pressing question was how might her life have played out had she and Garrett been given the opportunity to keep their son? Might they now be a mirror image of the happy family standing before them?

Most likely not. But she ached for that happy imaginary couple.

They rounded the block, stopping at five more homes before returning to Garrett's mother's.

Dina had decorated the small house with enough Christmas kitsch to open her own holiday-themed store. Most every flat surface had been covered with fake snow and held blinking or glowing elves, reindeer and Santas. The large tree in the living-room bay window was live and fragrant and held a dizzying amount of colorful lights and homemade ornaments. Eve recalled Garrett complaining about not having a live tree. Guess he'd gotten his way. A more formally decorated themed tree stood in the dining room. It had white lights and hundreds of angels and silver glass balls. Its beauty was mesmerizing and held Eve transfixed.

Behind her, Dina said, "Pretty amazing, huh? My grandmother gave me my first angel ornament when I was just eight years old. I've been collecting them ever since."

"That's incredible."

Waving off Eve's wonder, Dina said, "I'm sure you have way more impressive collections in that mansion of yours."

Eve shrugged. "They might be more expensive, but somehow yours seems more meaningful."

"If you don't mind my asking, how are you feeling these days? I've seen an awful lot of troubling Barnesworth business news in the paper."

"Don't remind me." Eve fingered a particularly delicate angel with a gold gossamer gown and feathered wings. "It'll get cleared up. We've weathered worse storms."

"Well…" Dina patted her back. "Garrett and I are here for you if you ever need us."

"Thank you." She wrapped the woman in a spontaneous hug. "That means a lot."

While Dina bustled off to assemble a dessert buffet, Eve stayed at the gathering's sidelines, taking it all in. With Bing Crosby crooning many of the carols they'd just sung and a fire crackling in the hearth, the scene was unbearably cozy. It made Eve almost dread returning to her cavernous home. Her dad had been a larger-than-life figure and while he'd been alive, he always had one guest or another. Now, with Juanita the only staff member who slept over, at times Eve craved the close confines of her old sorority room. At least there, she'd always been surrounded by people—maybe no one she felt particularly close to, but live bodies all the same.

"What's wrong?" Garrett asked, appearing by her side. "You're letting all of these women beat you to the cookies. At the rate they're scarfing them down, in another five minutes every damned one will be gone—the cookies, not the ravenous women."

He held a stack of four iced sleighs. Grinning, she noted, "Looks like my biggest competition is you."

"Have one." He held it to her lips. The unexpected intimacy brought a rush of heat, making her recall not the taste of sugar and icing, but the faint hint of beer riding his sexy breath.

When she bit the cookie, he smiled. His strong white teeth and the lazy draw of his lips set her pulse racing. A craving to kiss him swelled her breasts as if her body instinctively wanted him.

"Good, huh?" he asked, indicating to his mother's baking.

"Delicious," she answered, thinking of his lips.

Chapter Eight

"I'm sorry," the town librarian whispered to Garrett, "but we're closing early today for our Christmas party. You and Ms. Barnesworth will have to go."

"Sure. I understand." For the past three hours, he and Eve had searched computer archives of neighboring towns' birth announcements. As usual, with no results.

Eve groaned.

"Chin up," he said with what he hoped came across as a playful nudge. His elbow had grazed her right breast, reminding him all too well just how intoxicating her bare skin had felt against his. "Maybe on the way out we'll snag a few cookies."

"You're obsessed with cookies."

He grinned. "It's Christmas. Now that the whole Santa conspiracy is out of the box, baked goods are all I have."

She closed her eyes and sighed.

"What?" Despite having done his dead-level best to fatten her up, she still seemed frail. As if the slightest wisp of wind or more bad news would send her physically and emotionally toppling. He should've held on to his anger at her for not including him in all decisions concerning their son, but that brand of negative energy felt counterproductive. "Bummed about not finding any new leads?"

"Of course." She'd slung her purse over her shoulder. "The clock is ticking on how long you'll even be in town. If we don't find him by the end of your leave, where do we turn?"

"You worry too much. Let's just for now keep the status quo. We'll figure out the rest as we go along."

He pushed in their chairs, then ushered her from the quiet back room into the library's main room where a surprisingly raucous party was in full swing.

Telling himself he'd slipped his arm around her waist more for support than because of his craving to touch her, he whispered in her ear. "Who knew librarians like Aerosmith? Wanna crash?"

"*Everyone* likes Aerosmith," she teased.

"They've dimmed the lights," he noted, "the dessert table is unmanned and I'm pretty sure that table in front of periodicals is holding Rotel dip and Lit'l Smokies."

"I can do better. Come on." This time she took his hand, guiding him out to their respective cars. "Follow me to my place. Not only will I feed you, but we'll hatch up a fresh plan of attack."

"I don't know…" When he cocked his head, he reminded her of an incorrigible little boy. Which only made her wonder how adorable their son must be. Throat tight, she dropped his hand. "If there aren't baked goods involved, I'm not sure I'm on board."

"Th-that's okay. I probably should tackle more work anyway." Stupid. Why had she put herself out there like that? She should've known he'd want nothing more to do with her outside of this search for their son. What she couldn't have known was how badly his rejection would sting.

"What? It's past seven. Eve—I was joking. I'm so hungry I'd cheerfully eat an MRE."

"What's that?" She wrinkled her nose.

"Officially stands for Meal, Ready-to-Eat. But also affectionately called Meals Rejected by the Enemy or Mystery Meals. Either way, they pretty much suck. Promise, you could feed me a grilled cheese and I'd be forever in your debt."

"All right then…" Her heart skipped in ridiculous excitement. Lord knew, she'd have been better off had Garrett gone home to his mom's, so why did she now feel like the giddy teen she'd once been? Hoping to spend a few minutes after the big game with the star quarterback? "Let's go."

As tonight was Juanita's weekly canasta party, Eve and Garrett would have the house to themselves.

Eve beat him there, and used the time to light a fire and a few lamps and candles in the wood-paneled den—the only remotely cozy part of the house. She'd just made it to the kitchen when the doorbell rang.

She ran in that direction only to catch herself. The sudden movement brought on a dizzy spell that took a moment to pass. Though she hadn't been hungry for lunch, apparently her body was.

"Long time no see," Garrett quipped when she welcomed him through the front door. "Fixed anything to eat yet?"

"I've been home five minutes."

"And?" His smile made her weak all over again.

"Us Barnesworths aren't exactly known for our talents in the kitchen. But come on, and I'll see what I can do."

Twenty minutes later, Eve sat at the granite counter's bar, watching Garrett finish a divine-smelling cheese-and-veggie omelet. How was it that he was not only great at knocking out reporters, belting out carols and now even beating pancake batter? He'd never said much about his life as a SEAL, but she could only imagine he was equally as proficient at that, too. Was there anything the guy couldn't do?

"Voilà." He plated half the omelet, setting it in front of her with a napkin and fork.

"When did you learn to do all of this when here I thought you've been off fighting wars?"

He laughed. "It's no big deal—a fact you'd know if you hadn't lived your entire life as a pampered princess. Which begs the question, how did you and your ex survive when we've just witnessed the sad truth that you can't even crack an egg?"

"Stop!" She should've been outraged, but his ribbing was kind of fun. He spoke the truth and the fact that she had reached her twenties without learning even the most basic of cooking skills was admittedly sad. "I make a mean bowl of Cap'n Crunch—and nobody orders takeout faster than me."

The sweet vanilla scent of his pancakes made her stomach growl and for the first time in weeks, she felt truly hungry. After her first bite of omelet, she groaned with contentment. "This is so good."

"Thanks. Made these for my roomies all the time."

"Tell me about them." He flipped perfect pancakes.

"Deacon and I were together the longest, but he went and got married on me. Ellie's a great gal, though. They share a gorgeous little girl—Pia. Took them forever to get together, but now that they're finally official, they're rock solid."

"Sounds like a fairy tale." Eve hadn't meant it to be, but her tone was wistful. What must it be like? Sharing that perfect kind of love?

"It was—is." He handed her a stack of the sweet portion of their meal before turning introspective. "A while ago, I told Deacon about you getting pregnant back in high school. He's the only one who knows— aside from my folks."

"Wh-what exactly did you say?" Had he trashed her for shutting him out? If he had, could she blame him?

"His own daughter came as a surprise—complicated, but enough like our situation that I shared with him how I had a son, but he died. And I told him how I'd have given anything for not only our boy to have lived, but to get a second chance with you."

Eve's throat knotted.

"Now here we are, and it's…" Having loaded his own plate, he killed the flame on the stove, turning his back on her.

"Still complicated?"

"That's one way of putting it." He half laughed, but in doing so, met her eyes. In that one simple look he conveyed warmth and caring and strength beyond measure. "Truth is, once we find our boy, aside from our dealings with him, we most likely won't be in each other's lives."

Why? Eve wished she could give voice to the question, but lacked the courage. Beyond that, how did she begin explaining how much she enjoyed Garrett's company? And how already she dreaded his leaving after the holidays. "You're probably right."

"Any idea where Juanita keeps the syrup?"

"Your guess is as good as mine." Before, Eve had looked forward to her evening alone with Garrett. Now she wasn't sure what to expect. Part of her wanted to tell him everything, how their night spent caroling had meant so much. And how what had no doubt just been sex to him had been the first time she'd wholly felt pleasure in years. But she couldn't say any of that, because he wouldn't care and neither should she.

He found a glass jar filled with an amber liquid, pouring it into a saucepan. "Whenever Mom makes pancakes, she warms the syrup."

"Nice touch."

"How about you grabbing butter?" He winked. "I assume you know where that is?"

Had they still been sixteen, she'd have stuck out her tongue. As they'd both moved considerably past that stage, she merely slipped from her stool to do as he'd asked.

In the pass off, their hands brushed and sadly, the warm rush of awareness from his lightest touch was strong as ever. Had things been different between them, the night could've taken an entirely different turn— one she instinctively knew would fill her with deep satisfaction.

They ate in silence, and at the meal's end, restored Juanita's kitchen to its usual pristine state.

"Still feel up to talking strategy?"

"Sure." Eve dried her hands on a dishcloth.

He stood only a few feet from her, leaning against the granite counter, arms folded, legs crossed at the ankles.

His posture told her he'd shut down. But why? Before their meal, the mood had been lighthearted. Now she got the impression his being there was a chore.

"Everything okay?" she asked.

He nodded. "Why?"

She shrugged. "You seem different."

Sighing, he uncrossed his legs and leaned forward, bracing his hands on the center island. "Look, I guess for a few minutes there, the two of us felt good. Almost like we did back when we were a couple, but our lives are different now, and the last thing either of us needs is a complication like romance. It was no good for us back then and now…" He shook his head. "I'm stupid for even bringing it up."

"No, I feel the same," Eve somehow managed to choke out past the knot in her throat. But did she? She wasn't sure how she felt about anything anymore— least of all Garrett.

"Good." He sharply exhaled. "Now that that's out in the open, let's get back to our search. The newspaper thing was a bust, so now what? Got anything?"

What Eve had was a headful of confusion. A chest aching with yet another loss. But then it wasn't as if Garrett had ever been truly hers to begin with, so she needed to once and for all get over him. "Part of me is so exhausted, I wonder if we're just beating our heads against a wall? Realistically, what are our odds of finding him?"

"Forget the odds. Let's focus on the mission at hand." Garrett pulled her into a hug, which only compounded Eve's problems. Just because she didn't want to be attracted to him—*shouldn't* be attracted to him—didn't mean her body had gotten the memo.

"You're right. I'm just so tired."

Taking her hand and giving her an encouraging squeeze, he said, "Get a good night's rest and we'll re-group tomorrow. I've got a few Christmas gifts to pick up in the morning, but in the afternoon, let's get back to your dad's files. Sound okay?"

She nodded. "Thanks for dinner—" she waved her hands and added "—for everything. I'm not usually this wishy-washy."

"Give yourself a break. You just lost your father. You've been thrown into a new role as head of a huge company. The holidays are barreling toward us, and I don't know about you, but I have yet to buy a single present. You and I..." He blasted her with his grin. "Well, you and I had a nice but kind of surprising time that threw us both off our games."

"That's one way of putting it." Eve's grimace said it all. The emotional roller coaster she'd been on since Garrett had been thrust back into her life was anything but a game. Even if it were, she was definitely losing.

"You're home early."

Garrett shut the front door to find his mom seated on the floor, surrounded by wrapping paper, boxes and bows.

"Mind handing me the tape?" She nodded toward the coffee table, which was a good five feet from her base of operations. "Somehow it keeps escaping."

He handed it to her, then sidestepped her projects to collapse onto his dad's recliner.

"Before I forget, your friend Deacon called. When you get a chance, he'd like an update on your search."

Garrett laughed. "That makes two of us."

"Uh-oh." She filled out the gift tag on a rectangular red box. "I take it you and Eve didn't come up with any brilliant new ideas for finding your son?"

"We keep hitting dead end after dead end." What he had no intention of hashing over with his mother was just how good being with Eve was starting to feel. Cooking for her had felt so natural. Their teasing banter tasted better than any food ever had. He found himself craving her company, but how in his right mind could he want to be around a woman who would inevitably only bring him more pain? "At this point, Hal's files are our only possible lead. But there's about five thousand of them, so our progress has been slow."

"You'll get there," his mom assured him.

The house phone rang.

"Mind getting that?" Dina was stuck under his uncle Todd's sweater box.

On the phone, Grandma Fern was feeling chatty, so after a good ten minutes relaying to her his activities of the past few days—leaving out certain intimate details—Garrett passed off the phone to his mom.

Upstairs, seated on the foot of his bed, he hit the speed dial for Deacon's number on his cell. "Hey, man," he said when his friend answered on the third ring. "How's it going?"

"Hectic." Deacon chuckled. "Ellie's got a nasty case of holiday fever, plus my mom, real dad, stepsisters and Tom's folks will all be here for Christmas. I train like a dog all day, then come home to clean, wrap presents and bake cookies all night."

"Sorry to hear about the extra work, but sounds like you've finally got a handle on the whole family thing."

"I do, man, and it's great." Garrett could practically

see the size of his friend's smile over the phone. Deacon, Ellie and Pia made a great trio. Too bad their mutual friend Tom had had to die in order for that to happen.

"While I've got you—" Garrett reached for the photo of him and Eve taken after a particularly exciting football win against their rival town of Philmoore. The years had been kind to her. She was just as beautiful now as she'd been all those years ago. "Remember that talk we had about how around the holidays is the only time I think about what might've been between me and Eve had our son lived?"

"Yeah..."

"Well, Christmas is almost here and our son is alive and the more I'm with Eve, the more I—"

"You sleep with her?"

Garrett rubbed his hand over his whisker-stubbled jaw.

"I'll take that as a yes."

"It's been days now, but I can't get her out of my head. This woman crucified me. Besides, even if by some bizarre twist of fate we did hook up again, then what? She's the uppity CEO of *Daddy's* big business and I'm a SEAL with no desire to leave Virginia Beach."

In the background, Garrett heard Pia laugh. There was no better sound on earth than a child's laughter. Every day since learning his son was alive, Garrett had hoped for great happiness for his little boy.

"This may not be what you want to hear," Deacon said, "but it's high time I give you a dose of your own medicine."

Groaning, Garrett said, "I don't even remember what it was—and I'm not sure I want to know."

"Basically, you read me the riot act about getting to know Pia and being a great dad."

"What'd I say about Ell?" More than anything, Garrett wanted his old friend to reassure him. Tell him that once Garrett got back to base, the feel of Eve's lips against his would become at best, a hazy memory.

"Been a while," Deacon said with Pia giggling into the phone, "but best I can remember, you advised me to try us working everything out together."

For Deacon that advice had turned into relationship gold.

Problem was that when it came to Garrett and Eve, there wasn't even anything to work out. There was as of yet no son, and there sure as hell was no official *them*.

"BUT THERE IS *always* a Barnesworth Christmas party." Wearing her hair in what had now become her customary bun, Juanita chased Eve up the stairs to her room. It'd broken Eve's heart when Juanita admitted she no longer wore her wigs because she no longer had Hal around to tease her about them.

"Trust me, I think everyone who's usually invited will understand. Daddy's barely been in his grave a month." Two days had passed, during which she and Garrett had sifted through more than three hundred of her father's files apiece with still no leads bringing them closer to finding their son.

"But Miss Eve, party make you feel better. You see."

Having reached her room, Eve leaned against the doorjamb. "Please, Juanita, if you want to have a party so bad, then host one for your own family. Use the whole house. Have them stay over if you'd like. We sure have enough empty rooms."

"Oh, no," the housekeeper said with a firm shake of her head. "Mr. Hal would never agree."

"But he's not here and I am. You have my full blessing to hold the biggest, craziest, most wonderful holiday party you can imagine, only under one condition—leave me out of it."

Tears shone in Juanita's brown eyes. "Miss, no. We couldn't have party without you."

Eve took Juanita's hands, giving them a squeeze. "Sure you could—and you will. Just take whatever you need for food out of the household budget and while you're at it, pick up a few crazy-expensive electronic gadgets for those adorable great-nieces and nephews."

"What about you?" Concern shone in her eyes. "You can't just sit up here and be all by yourself for the holidays."

Eve hugged her dear friend. "I'll be fine."

"What about Mr. Garrett? You be with him for Christmas?"

Loving this dear woman all the more for her bungled English, it crushed Eve to realize for all practical purposes, Juanita was her only remaining family.

What about your son?

Eve wasn't sure whether the thought of him lost and alone somewhere hurt worse than the hope that he was well-adjusted and happy and an integral part of a loving family. The part of her wanting him to need her turned nauseous with guilt. On the other hand, if he'd already formed a rich life without her, she was once again on her own—the crushing weight of that thought made it hard to breathe.

"Mr. Garrett make for Christmas merry." Juanita winked. "He big muscles. *Muy caliente!*"

Very hot. Yep. That about summed up Garrett…

Cheeks flaming, Eve stopped just short of fanning herself from the memory of his bare skin pressed to hers.

Chapter Nine

"Thanks for coming with me." Tuesday afternoon, Eve and Darcie had been Christmas shopping for the past three hours in Coral Ridge's busiest shopping district. Fairview Plaza had been built around a landscaped lake and featured gift shops, restaurants and pricey boutiques. Even though the day was gorgeous with the temperature in the low seventies, a local high-school choir dressed in Victorian-period costume belted out carols. Behind them, ducks squawked over bread crusts being tossed by shrieking toddlers. Reminders of the season were all around them in ten-foot Christmas trees, each decked out with hundreds of colorful balls, draped boughs of lit greenery and of course, Santa's village complete with mechanical reindeer. "I've got a million things to do piled up at the office, but with the big day looming, I couldn't put this off any longer."

"Juanita's going to flip over her purse." Darcie sidestepped a duck who'd strayed from the flock. "Is that lady following us?"

"Who?" Eve peered over her shoulder, but Darcie stage-whispered for her not to look.

"That obviously dyed-redhead in the black shirtdress with the oversize vintage Chanel purse I would sell a kidney for. I swear she's been behind us through the last three stores and now out here, too."

Eve couldn't resist poking fun at her friend. "You been watching too much *Law & Order* again?"

"Is such a thing even possible?" Darcie glanced around for the mystery woman, but she was gone—just like Eve figured she would be. "Anyway, back to Juanita's purse, she's gonna love it."

"Hope so. She's been so kind…" Eyes tearing, Eve forced a deep breath. No more crying. "She deserves something extra special."

"That designer masterpiece certainly fits the bill. Now, you've covered most everyone at work and Juanita's extended family. Only person left—besides me—" Darcie winked "—is Garrett."

"Really? You think I should get him something?"

"You weren't planning on it?"

"No." They'd reached Eve's gold Jag and she popped the trunk. Matt had given her the car. She secretly thought it ostentatious, but it was paid for and got her from home to work just fine. "You think I should?"

"Will you see him Christmas Day?" Once Darcie added her few bags, they shut the trunk and climbed into the car.

"I don't think so."

"But you might?" Darcie had flipped down the sun visor and dabbed translucent powder to her glowing chin and forehead. At five she was meeting Chad from Accounting for drinks. As this was already their fourth date, Eve gathered it was going well.

"Oh, my God, does it matter?"

"You don't have to get snippy." After adding lipstick, Darcie asked, "What are you doing for Christmas?"

"Juanita's having a party at the house, so I'll probably load a plate with whatever delicious creations she makes, then hide out in my room, watching movies."

Darcie winced. "No *bueno*. How about coming to Miami with me? Mom says a megahottie moved into the condo down the hall from hers. Bet he's got equally hot friends."

Eve pulled from the shopping center's lot onto the main road. "Thanks, but I'm not really feeling up for much more than a nap. And I thought you were all hot and bothered about Chad?"

"I am, but a girl should keep her options open." Darcie spritzed herself with perfume. "As for spending Christmas with me and Leo and Mom, promise you'll at least think about it."

"HAVE YOU GIVEN ANY THOUGHT to inviting Eve here for the holiday?" Dina rolled out a pie crust, then lifted it to fit onto a plate.

"No." Truthfully, though Garrett knew he had to spend time with her to try finding their son, the last thing he wanted was the rest of his leave being haunted by her company. Because every second he was with her only served as a reminder of how much she'd once meant.

"If you won't, I will. Poor girl. Eve has her housekeeper, but aside from Juanita, now that her father's gone, Eve's an orphan."

"Okay, first—she's not a girl, but a woman. And second, with all due respect, Mom, please stay out of this. It doesn't concern you."

"This girl—woman—is the mother of my grandchild, so you'd better believe this concerns me." She slammed the same wooden rolling pin she'd been using since Garrett had been a child onto the counter. *"Greatly."*

Seated at the kitchen table, Garrett ran his hands over his face. Somehow, a mission to Somalia sounded a damned sight better than dealing with the mess he had going here at home.

"Your father and I never fought more than when you told us Eve was pregnant. I wanted to bring that poor child here, where she'd be looked after properly." She took a shuddering breath. "Your father told me to leave it alone. You had scholarship prospects for football and with all her family money, we knew wherever Hal had whisked her off to, she'd be fine."

"You keep referring to her as a girl, but, Mom—"

"Back then, that's all she was. A scared girl all of sixteen who had to have felt abandoned. I saw you hurting and knew she was probably feeling the same. And then when we heard the baby had died…" She silently cried and he went to her, curving his arm around her sagging shoulders. "Y-your dad felt the whole matter was behind us, but I knew this would leave you and Eve scarred for life. And me, too. I love babies and make no mistake yours would have been—*may still be*—loved."

"I know. You also have to know I'm fine." How easily the lies seemed to come. Lies to his mother about him being over the whole thing. Lies to himself about how much he still cared for Eve. But caring didn't equate to second chances or a renewed sense of trust. Caring didn't make his heart any less vulnerable to pain. He might've advised Deacon to run full speed ahead into his relationship with Ellie, but Garrett preferred keeping a safe distance from the woman who'd taught him that love was best left alone.

THAT NIGHT, GARRETT AND EVE had been at their continuing search through Hal's files for about an hour in her quiet office when his conscience got the better of him. "So look, Mom wants you to come for Christmas."

She didn't even put down her latest file. "And you?"

"What do you mean?"

Face still hidden behind a manila folder, she asked, "Do *you* want me to share the day with you and your family?"

Yes. Not really. Hell, honestly, he didn't have a clue.

At his expression, she said, "Thank you, but I already have plans." Her tone painfully formal, she moved on to the next pile stacked beside her.

"No, you don't."

"Oh, so first you issue an invitation your mom asked you to deliver, then you accuse me of lying?"

Garrett smacked his palm to the table. "It's not like that, and you know it— Sorry. Just sometimes your hoity-toity, Little Miss Perfect routine ticks me off. Don't you ever just belt out what you feel?"

"I—I feel grateful for your mother kindly thinking of me, but as for anything else..." She shrugged.

Hands braced on the table, he leaned across to kiss her. He kissed her hard. As far from polite as he knew how. And only when he'd had his fill of her taste and smell did he back away, already wanting more.

"I probably should apologize for that, too, but I'm not."

Fingers pressed over kiss-swollen lips, she shook her head. "No apology necessary. I, ah, okay, wow..." She bowed her head, but Garrett swore he spied a grin.

"For the record, I was taught from a very young age that it's crass to just blurt out whatever's on my mind. But since you appear interested, Juanita has invited her entire family to celebrate at our house—meaning it's not an impossibility that a couple hundred people and a Cuban band could show up at my door. As I'm craving a low-key, traditional ham and trimmings, I'd very much enjoy celebrating with your family—but only if you want me there."

Considering the kiss they'd just shared, of course Garrett wanted to see her every minute of every day, but Christmas was personal. It conveyed an emotional depth he wasn't sure he'd ever be capable of feeling.

"Should I take your silence as a no?"

He tilted his head back and sighed. "Would you believe me if I told you I don't know what I want? That it's complicated?"

Laughing, she said, "Complicated? That's the understatement of the century." She slid the file she'd been reading before their kiss across the table. "As if whatever's going on between us isn't enough to handle, take a look at this—pay special attention to the date."

Centered in the folder's crease was an age-faded canceled check. A check for a hundred grand made out to Joan Smith. The date just happened to be a couple days after their son's supposed death. "Whoa…"

"I know, right? Here we've been thinking Daddy sold our baby, but what does this mean? Why would he have paid someone that much money when on the black market, there's no telling how much he could've gotten?"

HEAD POUNDING, NAUSEOUS and exhausted, Eve stopped by the drugstore on her way home from the office. No doubt stress was making her feel as if she'd been hit by a dump truck, but then Garrett's kiss might also have something to do with her swimming head.

How could she be so incredibly physically attracted to him, when they no longer worked on an emotional level? Would *never* work. Her brain understood, so why couldn't her body figure it out?

A cold rain fell, so she hustled getting from her car inside. The pharmacy was loaded with parents and coughing kids and last-minute gift-seekers. With only one checkout clerk, the line was six deep.

Eve flipped through a magazine, but then looked up when she felt someone staring. She made brief eye contact with the redhead she'd have sworn was the same one Darcie had seen at Fairview Plaza. She may not have given the encounter a second thought save for the vintage Chanel purse Darcie had been crazy for. For any purse lover, it was truly exquisite. There couldn't be that many in the state—let alone Coral Ridge.

Eve moved up in line.

When a second glance over her shoulder showed the woman gone, Eve chastised herself for being as overly suspicious as her friend. It was a small town. People ran into each other all the time.

Once home, Eve ran a bath, and when she'd finished, and Juanita hassled her about eating, she took her dinner of grilled salmon, wild rice and a salad on a tray in bed. She couldn't remember ever having been so exhausted except when— No.

It couldn't be possible.

Fate wouldn't be so cruel.

Easing her hands beneath her floral comforter, slipping them under the waistband of satin pajama pants, she cupped her womb, wondering, fearing, praying there could once again be life inside.

"WOULD YOU DO ME A HUGE favor?" Eve asked Darcie at the office Wednesday morning. After a successful news conference, reporting that a third of the illegal immigrants her father had hired now had received expedited green cards, her nerve was bolstered enough to tackle the next item on her to-do list.

"Anything." Darcie typed out a few words on her keyboard. "Let me finish these last lines and I'll be right with you."

Pulse racing, Eve turned toward her own office. "If you're busy, we'll do this some other time."

"I'm good to go." Rotating on her desk chair to face Eve, she asked, "Want to revise this morning's official press release?"

"Not exactly..." Part of Eve felt embarrassed for what she needed her friend to do. Another part, an infinitely deeper portion of herself, had been burned so many times, she was afraid to hope there was cause to involve Darcie.

"What, then? I'm at your disposal."

"Thanks. I, ah..." On the verge of passing out due to her elevated heart rate, Eve figured it was now or never that she made her request. "Um, if you have time, I need you to run with me to the drugstore, then stand by for moral support."

Darcie's complexion turned gray. "Are you sick? Is this something serious you haven't told me about?"

"Possibly," Eve admitted, "but not in the way you think."

"Okay, then please enlighten me, because at the moment, you're kind of freaking me out."

Eve blurted, "I might be pregnant."

"What?" Darcie's shriek warranted her immediately covering her mouth. "Sorry," she whispered. "No way? You and Garrett? From just that one night?"

"It's probably in my head." Eve's headache had returned with a vengeance. "I'm barely a week late, but the only times I've ever felt this bone-deep tired have been—"

"Enough said." Darcie snagged her purse and two Snickers bars from her bottom desk drawer. Handing one candy bar to Eve, she said, "Let's ride."

FORTY-FIVE MINUTES LATER, Eve shared her office couch with Darcie, her still-blank pregnancy test on the coffee table in front of them. Mouth dry, heartbeat drumming out of control, Eve wasn't sure she'd survive the two minutes the test required.

Darcie asked, "How long has it been?"

"Thirty seconds."

"I'm sure it's been longer. Think the timer on your phone is broken?"

Eve checked. "Unfortunately, no."

With seconds ticking away, Eve was grateful when Darcie took her hand, delivering a squeeze.

"No matter what," her friend said with a reassuring smile, "everything's going to work out fine."

"Promise?" Even though the question was ridiculous in light of the fact she, more than anyone, knew life didn't come with guarantees, Eve appreciated Darcie's strong nod.

The timer on her phone dinged.

"I'm afraid to look." Eve had long since closed her eyes and her palms were sweating.

"What are you hoping for? Preggers or simple stress exhaustion?" Darcie asked.

"Not sure." *Liar.* Honestly, Eve deeply, truly wanted a baby. As for how she felt about once again sharing that miracle with Garrett? The verdict was still out.

"Well, you might want to decide sooner as opposed to later."

"Why's that?" Eve's eyes were still closed.

Then she was nearly toppled over by the force of Darcie's hug. "Because, sweetie, in nine short months you're going to be a mom!"

"YOU OKAY?" WEDNESDAY afternoon, Garrett sat next to Eve in the reception area of First National Bank & Trust, waiting to speak with the president about her father's mystery check. "Your color seems *off*."

"Thanks." Her look could've killed.

"Not that I'm not feeling that black dress," he back-pedaled, "just that it's such a nice day and all, I thought you might've worn something a little brighter. I like you in colorful stuff—not that I pay attention to that kind of stuff—clothes and stuff, just—"

Adopting her hoity-toity manner that never failed to annoy him, she asked, "You are aware you've used *stuff* three times in the same sentence?"

"Does it matter?" He wished he didn't care that the reasoning behind his words was that when she wore bright colors, she struck him as being more approachable. In black, she became the all-business ice princess he had no more in common with than Donald Trump.

"I suppose not." With her arms folded and her legs

politely crossed at the ankles, everything about her shut him out. Why was it, then, he so badly wanted in? Just the other night, his stolen kiss had been an incredible turn-on. The sex before that—insane. Did she not feel the same? The way even now, casually seated in adjoining chairs, their bodies practically hummed?

"Mr. Solomon. Ms. Barnesworth." The president, Jim Strong, extended his hand for both of them to shake. Garrett couldn't tell if his shock of black hair was a toupee, but his smile seemed genuine and his handshake was as strong as any SEAL's. To Eve, the banker said, "I was so sorry to hear of your father's passing. His service was deeply touching. He was a loyal customer for many years." Gesturing for Eve to lead the way into his office, Jim ushered the couple inside an oak-paneled space featuring plenty of family photos and three double-hung windows overlooking the south corner of city hall. Despite nonsmoking laws, sweet pipe smoke lingered in the air.

"Thank you." Eve took one barrel-shaped guest chair. Garrett took the other.

"As I imagine you're ready to get straight to business, I wish I had better news." From behind his desk, Jim fingered the check Eve had earlier had messengered over. "Unfortunately, as we might've guessed from the recipient's name—Joan Smith—tracking her down was a total dead end. She was never an account holder and as I'm sure you're aware, Ms. Barnesworth, as your father kept personal accounts well in excess of eight figures, the amount was never even questioned. The recipient was given the funds in cash. Now, for tax implications, I hope you don't mind, but as we're all old golfing buddies, I took the liberty of phoning your father's personal accountant, Cliff Stafford, and he said Hal claimed this amount as a charitable gift."

Leaning forward, Garrett asked, "So that means it went to an organization?"

Jim winced. "Not exactly. Apparently, Hal refused to disclose the name of the charity, so Cliff didn't allow the deduction. Now, what made the incident especially stand out in Cliff's mind was the fact that ordinarily, any time he denied your dad a deduction, Hal pitched a good old-fashioned fit. I loved Hal like a brother, but when it came to dealing with money, he could sometimes blow like a hurricane. In this instance, according to Cliff, your dad never so much as flinched about having his deduction denied." Sliding the check across the desk toward Eve, Jim continued, "We're all rather stumped. I even asked some of the tellers who were with us at the time the check was cashed, and all they remember is that the recipient was a woman, wearing an obvious blond wig, covered by a scarf. As this was a large sum of money and Hal is—was—our largest single depositor, his writing a check for this large a sum to an unknown woman wagged some tongues. This poorly disguised woman offered an apparently valid state ID bearing the name Joan Smith and placed the bundled cash in a Neiman Marcus shopping bag. That was that."

Garrett glanced to Eve to find her eyes shining.

Upset to have hit another dead end? Or that her father had been caught in one more lie? As she wore her best stone-faced expression, he'd never know.

"Again, I'm very sorry." Jim stood. "I'd hoped to be able to help provide whatever information you're needing."

"It's all right." Eve stood, extending her hand. She'd

already tucked the check into her purse. "Thank you for your time."

In Garrett's Mustang a few minutes later, he found Eve's vanilla expression beyond annoying. "That was total BS. I think he's hiding something."

"What gave you that idea?" She dug in her purse for a mint.

"Because he should've had more on this mystery woman. I thought with that much cash, somebody needed to be notified? DEA? FBI? At the very least, the IRS?"

She chewed her peppermint. "They probably were notified, but under the woman's real name. Her only crime was in using what I'm guessing was a false ID. Although just to be safe, want to do a quick search for Joan Smith?"

"No, dammit." Garrett hit the heel of his hand on the steering wheel. "What I want is for one thing to go right." He wanted Eve to show the same passion in searching for their son as she'd shown that morning on TV, during her news conference. What he craved most of all was to be able to trust her like he had when they'd been sixteen. People—his friends and parents—told him he'd been crazy for claiming to feel real love for Eve. They'd been kids. But he'd known. As a logical man who dealt in tangible evidence, there was no other explanation for why only she had held the capability to hurt him this bad. He'd loved her with every breath of his being and she'd dumped him like a proverbial bad habit. She'd dumped him and now here he sat, too many years later, in a stupid parking lot still as furious as the day he'd first learned she was gone. "I need just one damned thing to go right."

"Relax." She reached out to him, holding his clenched hand. Her touch acted as a balm and his breathing deepened. He hated that she held that power over him. "We *will* find our son. Apparently, not today, but even finding the check was a break. We're not even halfway through Daddy's files. Just think what else we may stumble across."

"I'm not used to stumbling."

"I know. Me, neither, but sometimes you have to adjust."

He growled.

Chapter Ten

Two days before Christmas, Eve had managed to snag someone else's cancellation appointment with her gynecologist. Having lost two babies and had one stolen, she wasn't taking any chances with this current miracle growing inside.

"This is a pleasant surprise." Dr. Seymour bustled into the small, homey room with Eve's chart in her hand. The doctor, with her long, blond hair, was an aging hippy and fought technology. The offices as a whole were done in bright '70s colors with plenty of posters bearing happy families, peace signs and rainbows. "When my nurse told me you're here for a pregnancy test, I did a double take to ensure I had the right file."

Face flushed, Eve fanned herself. "I surprised myself with this one."

"How about the baby's father? He excited?"

Wincing, Eve admitted, "He doesn't know."

"Ah—" the doctor smiled "—planning a romantic surprise announcement?"

"Something like that." Eve fought the childish urge to cross her fingers while lying. Of course, she'd tell Garrett, but in her own time. She'd suffered two miscarriages. Keeping this baby a secret until he or she successfully made it at least into the second trimester hurt no one.

"I love a good surprise. I told Randy about our fourth daughter while snorkeling in St. Thomas. Best day ever."

Knowing her experience with Garrett wouldn't be anywhere near that special, Eve just smiled.

"As I'm sure you knew, our test was also positive, but considering your history, please take care of yourself. Eat right. Drink plenty of fluids. No twelve-hour days at the office. In fact, now would be a great time to delegate. All that said, I don't want to frighten you. Just because you've had a miscarriage in the past doesn't mean you can't have a perfectly healthy baby now."

Shoulders sagging in relief, Eve fought tears.

"Hey…" The doctor rubbed her back. "With losing your dad and the recent fuss at your company, you've been through a lot. Give yourself permission to take it easy and enjoy this pregnancy. You deserve all the happiness a baby can bring."

DR. SEYMOUR'S OFFICES were on the third floor of a medical complex. Upon reaching the lobby, Eve made a brief stop in the restroom before heading to her car.

A sudden breeze caught the pamphlets the nurse had given her, along with a vitamin sample pack from her purse's side pocket. When she knelt to pick it all up, a reflection caught her eye. Seated on a bench not ten feet away was the woman who carried the vintage Chanel. At first glance, to the average onlooker, she seemed to be checking her makeup, but as she had the night in the pharmacy, Eve couldn't shake the feeling the woman had been watching her.

Pregnancy hormones already getting the better of her?

She would've assumed so, but then the woman abruptly stood before jogging to meet her. "Ms. Barnesworth?"

"Y-yes…" Eve wasn't sure whether to talk to the woman or call for help. As the building entrance was full of people and the woman didn't seem threatening, Eve asked, "Can I help you?"

"No. My name is Tina Northridge and I—I'd just like to pay my condolences. Your father once did me a great kindness and out of respect for him, since I thought I recognized you, I—well, this seemed like the perfect opportunity."

The woman's demeanor seemed *off*. She fidgeted to an abnormal degree. Nervous? "I, um, saw you with a man at the library last week. Find what you were looking for?"

Alarm bells rang in Eve's head. "How exactly did you know my father?"

"Doesn't matter," Tina said with an exaggerated smile. "I should get going, but it was nice talking with you." As suddenly as she'd entered Eve's afternoon, she left it, scurrying off to a car far across the lot. Before Eve thought to get the tag number of the woman's dark sedan, she was gone.

"SORRY TO DROP IN ON YOU without calling," Eve said to Dina fifteen minutes later, "but I have to see Garrett."

"Of course, come in." She stepped aside, but not before casting Eve a worried look. "Everything okay?"

"Truthfully—" a small laugh escaped her "—I'm not sure."

"We all have days like that. Garrett, honey? You

have company!" Snatching a foil-wrapped chocolate from a bowl on the entry-hall table, Dina said to Eve, "I think he's in the office—what'd he call it? Skipping with his friends?"

"Skyping?" Eve suggested.

"That's it." Even though Coral Ridge was experiencing Florida at her winter best, Dina had managed to make her home feel like Christmas. Beyond her two trees and the decorations she'd already had up the last time Eve had been by, she'd added a miniature holiday village complete with twinkling lights and twirling ice skaters. Cinnamon laced the air, making Eve's typically nauseous stomach growl. "Did my son remember to invite you for Christmas dinner?"

"He did, thank you."

"Well?" She knelt to pick up an ornament that'd fallen from her live tree. "Fat Albert thinks my decorations are his toys. Anyway, can I set a place for you at dinner?"

Eve knew the prudent answer would be no, but the house was so cozy and Dina so warm and inviting that Eve nodded. "Thank you. I'd love to share your meal."

"Good."

Was it? Especially considering the secret gift Eve carried? Dina would be elated to learn she'd soon have a grandchild, but fear kept Eve from sharing her news. She'd already lost three children and her heart couldn't yet again bear that kind of pain.

"We'll have fun. Plus, my sister's making her cranberry cheesecake. It's to die for— Garrett!"

"What, Mom? I'm on the phone!"

"Eve's here!"

"If he's busy I can…" Eve hooked her thumb over her shoulder, already turning for the door.

"Hey." Garrett emerged from the hall wearing khaki cargo shorts and nothing else. His chest was broad enough for its own zip code and her mouth dried. "Let me grab a shirt and I'll be right out."

Was a shirt really necessary? "Okay. Fine."

"Cookie?" Dina held out a tray of frosted angel-shaped cookies. Funny, though, how the naughty thoughts racing through Eve's mind were far from angelic.

"Thank you." Eve took two.

After having one for herself, Dina said, "Sorry to leave you, but I have a date with my most ornery flowerbed."

"Before you go," Eve asked, "should I bring anything on Christmas?"

Garrett's mother ambushed Eve in a welcomingly tender hug. "Just your smiling self."

"How long have you been here?" Garrett regrettably had added a white T-shirt to his outfit.

"Long enough for your mom and I to have a nice chat."

He groaned. "That can't be good."

"It was." She grabbed more cookies from the counter. "I'd forgotten how much I like her—and her sweets."

"She likes you, too."

Eve had hurried over to tell Garrett her news, but she now felt tongue-tied and awkward. Her attraction for him distracted her from her primary goal of finding their son. And it had to stop. Only with another child of his growing inside her, she not only craved being with him, but being held by him. Kissed by him. Made love to by...

Eve's cheeks flamed.

"You overheated?" he asked. "With all of Mom's Christmas gear going, it gets pretty warm."

Hands to her cheeks, she shook her head. "No, that's far from my problem." Thankful for the segue, though not for any reason he might imagine, Eve relayed her interaction with Tina Northridge. "So you can see, when she asked if I'd found what I was looking for, why I'm wholly convinced she knows exactly what—or rather, whom—we're seeking."

"Whoa..." He stepped backward to lean against the kitchen island's butcher-block counter. "Wish you'd gotten her license-plate number, but that's okay. These days, practically all you need is a name to find out someone's entire life story. Anyway—" His grin was already intoxicating, but then he pulled her into an impromptu hug. He drew back to face her, as if intending to further celebrate with a kiss, but then released her, combing his fingers through his hair. "This is huge."

"Yes." For so many more reasons than he thought. Mostly, she realized with a sad twinge, because as soon as they found their son, this forced closeness would no longer be necessary. And of course, he'd have a relationship with their new son or daughter, but that was far different from him sharing anything of true meaning with her.

"Excited?" Garrett had asked an old football buddy of his who was a city cop to run Tina's name. Now, the afternoon before Christmas, he and Eve stood on Tina's front porch in Lakewood—a town fifty miles from Coral Ridge. Though they had her phone number, they'd decided an in-person meeting might prove more beneficial. "Our son could be inside."

"I'm excited and a little scared—but mostly excited." She visibly swallowed hard.

"Know the feeling." Forcing a breath, he rang the bell. "Here goes..."

After a few minutes, the front door of the well-maintained two-story home opened as far as the chain latch allowed. All he could see of the woman before him was a shock of white hair, narrowed, wary eyes, a black Nike jogging suit and a bedazzled cane. "Yes?"

From behind him, Eve whispered, "That's *not* her."

"Ah, hello, ma'am." Garrett had a tough time speaking past the emotional knot blocking his throat. He introduced himself and Eve to the elderly woman, then asked, "We've come to see Tina. Is she here?"

"All right."

"Tina Northridge. This is her address?"

"That's me. But I don't know you, and I'm not looking to buy anything."

"Oh, no, we're not looking to sell. Just for some information." He gave her the highlight reel. "So you can see, any help you might be able to give, we'd greatly appreciate."

Still not fully opening the door, Tina said, "Sorry, but I don't know anything about this woman using my name. Wish I did. You seem like a nice couple and I've always enjoyed solving a good mystery."

"Yes, well..." It took every shred of the manners Garrett's mom had taught him not to punch the woman's brick wall in frustration. "We're sorry to have bothered you. Thanks for your time."

In the car, silence hung heavy between him and Eve. Ten miles down the road, she started crying.

Garrett knew he should pull over, comfort her with a hug, but he was upset, too. Just like he'd been when she'd taken off with his child in her womb and returned home with nothing—not even the smallest shred of sympathy for him and what he'd lost. From the first moment she'd told him they were expecting, he'd stupidly been happy. He'd believed the two of them could conquer anything together. And they could've. If only she'd given him a chance.

"W-we need to give up." Crying all the harder, digging through her purse, then pulling out tissue, she blew her nose. "I can't take this disappointment anymore. M-my chest felt near exploding from anticipation, and then bam—just like always when I w-want something, it's gone."

"I'm sorry, Eve, but knock it off. I'm not a quitter and neither are you."

"You're horrible." She'd curled onto her side. She'd grown so thin, from this angle she could've again been that slight girl he used to love.

He tightened his grip on the wheel. "Maybe so, but there's no way in hell I'm ever giving up on our son."

"You think I want to?" She'd faced him, tears streaming down her pale cheeks.

Her frailty made him feel like the world's biggest ass. Was he wrong to still be angry with her over something that'd been nearly as much out of her control as it had his? "My God, Garrett, cut me some slack. I'm not a freakin' SEAL. It's only been a few weeks since I lost my best friend and hero—only to find out Hal wasn't anywhere near the man I'd built him up to be. I've got other things I'm dealing with, too, and most days I'm doing good just to get out of bed. I feel like an emotional leaf, on the verge of crumbling or skittering away in the wind. The last thing I need right now is your gung ho, hoorah I-don't-quit crap."

"Screw you."

"Screw me?" She laughed, but the borderline hysterical sound made his stomach uneasy. He'd gone too far and he was sorry. "Oh, seems like we've already tried that a few times and it never really works out."

EVE SAT AT THE SOLOMON family Christmas meal, mentally drifting as if in a dream. She wasn't even sure why she'd come. Mainly because she'd told Dina she would and always honored her word. Then there was the fact that Juanita had been so excited to share this day with her family that the last thing Eve wanted was to hang around there being a wet blanket. Her housekeeper— her friend—would never have let her spend the day alone in her room, and the Solomon house, though by no means quiet, was infinitely more peaceful than the *two* Cuban bands Juanita had hired.

Bing Crosby crooned carols on the living-room stereo and since the day outside was gorgeous with temperatures in the mid-seventies, the only fire crackling played on Dina's TV.

"So I was talking with another teacher on recess duty the other day—" Garrett's aunt Carol leaned closer to Eve while taking a yeast roll from a basket "—and she told me the Barnesworth Shoe Factory was opening an outlet store for all those fancy designer shoes y'all are making. That true?"

"Sadly, no." Eve used her fork to shuffle her green-bean casserole from one clear spot on her plate to another. Luckily, no one sat on her other side. "We only make the shoes for the big-name designers. We don't own the actual shoes, which means we don't have the right to sell them."

Carol smoothed butter onto her roll. "Well, if any accidentally fall off a conveyor belt, you know where to find me."

"Sorry to disappoint you again," Eve said with a faint laugh, "but they're all handmade."

"That's what I figured, but it never hurts to try." She closed her eyes while enjoying her roll. "Mmm. Dina makes the best rolls on the planet. Want another?"

"No, thanks." Since her latest round with Garrett, Eve's appetite had been even less than normal. Worry for her baby—*his baby*—consumed her. She couldn't live through losing another child. Part of her wanted so badly to tell him about her pregnancy, but why? He'd proven during their visit to the wrong Tina he couldn't be depended upon for support.

That's not fair.

Damning her conscience, Eve's mind regretfully replayed the times Garrett had been achingly sweet and supportive. The afternoon he'd carried her from her father's funeral and held her while she cried in the shower. Garrett was a good man—just not for her. The two of them were too different in too many important ways.

She looked at him, thankfully seated two chairs from her on the opposite side of the table. Engrossed in a conversation about the latest Middle East peace treaty, his expression was as serious as it had been the other day in his car. Though he was handsome in any situation, she liked him best smiling. Cupping her belly, she warmed. This little life inside her just had to live.

"You all right?" Carol took her third roll. "You're awfully quiet over there. Need more green beans or ham?"

When Carol offered to serve her, Eve shook her head. "Thanks, but I'm already stuffed."

"You've hardly eaten. Ask me—not that you did—you're a little on the thin side."

Eve wasn't sure how to reply.

"Funny thing about you, Eve, I think the whole town feels a little proprietary and protective. Your dad having been mayor for so long, with you always at his side, you've grown up in front of us."

Again, Eve was speechless.

"Lay off, Mom." Carol's son, Zane, wadded his red cloth napkin, pitching it at her from across the dining-room table. "You spend too much time meddling in everyone's business."

"I do not," Carol argued. "Is it wrong for me to care?"

Down the table, Garrett had his phone in hand. "Excuse me. I have to get this."

With Garrett out of the room, his mother said, "I'm worried sick that's his team lead. He's been on the phone with him a few times in the past couple days."

Eve's throat tightened.

It was one thing knowing Garrett was a SEAL, but with him safe in Coral Ridge, the reality of what that meant hadn't sunk in.

"Eve?" Dina rose. "Honey, you look—"

THOUGH IT'D BEEN A FEW HOURS since his mom had screamed for him to come quick, Garrett still sat on the living-room sofa with sleeping Eve's head resting on his lap.

All present had wanted to call an ambulance—at the very least take Eve to the E.R.—but she'd insisted her fainting spell was due to a lack of food and sleep. Toss in her father's death and the search for their son and she was admittedly having a rough time.

Garrett stroked her hair.

He should never have gone off on her the way he had after their encounter with the wrong Tina. Not that it was an excuse, but he was so damned frustrated with everything. Not just the half-dozen false leads they'd trailed, but his whole relationship with Eve. After all they'd shared, he'd hoped they could at least be friends, but even that seemed in jeopardy.

And now he'd been called out on a mission.

And for the first time since earning his trident, he didn't want to go.

Chapter Eleven

While the rest of his family helped Garrett's mom clean the kitchen, Eve stood with him on the front porch. Not only was she still consumed with embarrassment over fainting at the table, but she was also filled with fear. First thing in the morning she'd camp at her doctor's until there was an opening in her schedule. Until then, the news that Garrett was headed into the heart of danger wasn't setting well. As much as she'd be almost grateful for him to be gone, she'd also be worried for his safety.

"Promise you'll start taking better care of yourself."

She nodded. "You, too. Know how long you'll be gone?"

"Nope. Even if I did, I couldn't tell you."

"Okay, then..." She edged toward her car. There was so much she wanted to say, but didn't know how. Considering the danger factor of his job, she should tell him they were having a second baby, but the words wouldn't come out. As desperately as she wanted—needed—this child, what if he didn't? What if he did and that opened a whole new can of custody worms? Worst of all, what if she told him, then lost the baby? No. It would be best to keep this to herself for now. With all her heart, she fought a crazy yearning to crush him in a hug. "I'm going to let you get packed."

He walked her to her car. "Eve?"

"Yes?" She met his gaze, but he looked away.

"Nothing. Sorry your holiday was cut short. If you'd like, I'm sure Mom wouldn't mind you staying. We usually play board games after dinner. Trivial Pursuit. Monopoly."

From somewhere inside, Eve found her smile. "Thank you, but I'm going to turn in early."

"Probably a good idea."

There was so much more she wanted to say, but even if she had the courage, now wasn't the time. He needed his mind clear to come safely home to his mother, hopefully his son, his new child.

And her?

Eve refused to even entertain the notion.

FORTY-EIGHT HOURS LATER, Garrett huddled in a musty-smelling cave just east of Pungsan, North Korea, with his teammates and best buds, Deacon and Tristan. Before stumbling across the shelter, he'd barely caught the shallow cave through his night-vision goggles because the snow had fallen so hard.

They'd rocked up the entrance, leaving a peephole large enough for a scope, then set up camp by the light of red-lens flashlights.

"See anything?" Tristan, a fellow good old boy from the Deep South, was on KP duty, assembling field supply rations for all three of them.

Deacon grunted. "Couldn't see a roach if it bit my eye."

"Where'd this storm even come from?" Garrett dried

and cleaned weapons. "It sure as hell didn't show up on the long-range forecast."

"We're not exactly in The Weather Channel's happy place."

"Yeah," Tristan argued, "but our guys usually get it better than this. I mean, you'd think we could tell the difference between flurries and a blizzard on radar?"

"Who knows." Garrett had finished with his M14 and moved on to Deacon's MK43.

Tristan asked, "You two want Mexican or Italian for dinner?"

"Neither," Garrett and Deacon said in unison.

Huddled around an MSR stove, the three men ate in silence, doused in the flashlights' eerie red glow. Garrett found his thoughts drifting to Eve. A day behind him in time, what was she doing? Was she thinking of him?

Deacon asked, "How's the search for your son?"

Garrett sucked the last of his hot sauce from the plastic packet, then filled both his friends in on the latest. "Not gonna lie, I was pretty bummed about Tina being another dead end, but Eve took it especially hard. She's scary thin and fainted on Christmas."

Tristan stuck a twig in the meager flame. "That's not cool. She okay?"

"I guess." Outside, wind howled and for all he knew, a North Korean army detail stood ten feet away, but all Garrett seemed capable of focusing on was the memory of how scared he'd been after Eve's collapse. He asked Deacon, "How did you know you were falling for Ellie?"

"That's tough..."

Tristan rolled his eyes. "Holy hell, I'll be glad to

get away from you two. Remember the good old days when we talked strippers, weapons and video-game strategies?"

"Just wait." Deacon elbowed the youngest of the group. "One of these days you're going to meet a woman you crave more than a cheeseburger after six months in Afghanistan."

"Screw love." Tristan pitched a pebble at the cave's far wall. "It's great in the moment, but when you lose it, it hurts like hell."

Deacon winced. "Well, there's one way of looking at it, but to answer your question—" he turned to Garrett "—I knew I had it bad for Ell when being without her hurt worse than being with her."

Garrett laughed. "Swell. Last time Eve about killed me by taking off and then not talking to me for damn near a decade. After that, still can't say I totally trust her. So, Tristan buddy, I'm siding with you. Love sucks."

Garrett slapped Tristan's hand in a high five.

They ate the rest of their meals in silence save for the wind. Only Garrett's mind wasn't all that quiet. Deacon might've meant his answer to be flippant, but the truth was, Garrett had thought of nothing but Eve and their missing son since setting foot in this country— a bad thing considering a big chunk of the world had a stake in whether or not they found and disabled the nukes intel had reported.

"Last girl I was with—" Tristan made a makeshift toothpick from his hot-sauce packet. "That nurse? Damn near lost my mind from her complaining. Turn out the light, get her more beer, take away a pillow, add one— Ask me, women are more trouble than they're—"

Tristan was cut off by their rock wall being kicked in.

A FEW DAYS AFTER CHRISTMAS, Dr. Seymour smiled upon hearing Eve's baby's heartbeat. "Though you're thinner than I'd like, this little guy or gal seems fine."

Eve exhaled. "You don't know how worried I've been."

"I can imagine. Sorry I was out of town. Next time you have a problem, go to the E.R." The doctor used a towel to clean lubricant from Eve's belly, then removed her gloves to make a note in Eve's chart. "And while I'm in lecture mode, do me and your kiddo a favor and take better care of yourself. Eat, drink, *rest*."

Nodding, Eve was still too emotionally charged to speak.

"Although seems like you promised to do all of that at your last appointment, so my faith in you being able to follow orders is dwindling."

Hands curved over her still-flat stomach, Eve said, "This time, I promise to put nothing before keeping myself and my baby healthy."

Armed with pregnancy-nutrition pamphlets and more vitamin samples, Eve stood at the office checkout desk, scheduling her next appointment, when a woman entered the waiting room. Only it wasn't just any woman, but Garrett's mom. And before Eve could discreetly vanish into the restroom, Dina flashed a friendly wave.

"This is a nice surprise."

Eve returned Dina's hug.

Dina asked, "Seeing the doctor about your fainting spell?"

"Um, yes. But I'm fine. Just like I thought, I'm not getting enough rest." Eve adjusted her pamphlets. Would it be too obvious if she shoved them in her purse?

"That's a relief. You scared the plum pudding out of

us at Christmas." Making a face, Dina laughed. "Now that I think about it, not a pretty image, but really, you gave us a fright. Glad you're okay."

Garrett's mom went in for another hug, only Eve was so nervous about Dina seeing her pamphlets, she ended up dropping them.

"I'm sorry." Dina knelt to pick them up. And then she read the covers. "'Eating for Two'? 'Mealtime for Mamas'? Eve, are you...?"

GARRETT ROLLED TO HIS LEFT, in the same motion, grabbing his 9 mm and firing off three rounds. He heard a grunt and thump, then nothing.

"Talk to me, guys..." Tristan had kicked out the stove, in the same motion, burying the flashlight. They now sat in total darkness, the cave silent save for an echoing drip.

"I'm behind you on the left," Deacon whispered. "Can you reach my MK? It's got our best scope."

Garrett inched forward, only to be barraged by enemy fire.

A string of curses and God's grace were the only things that got him back to Deacon and Tristan.

Momentarily safe behind a rock outcropping twenty feet deeper into the cave, Garrett didn't like being caged in. On the flip side, they held the power-position for picking off their shooters.

What if I—we—don't make it out of here? Who's going to find my son? Make sure Eve doesn't starve herself to death?

"What've you got?" Garrett forced himself to ask Deacon, who stared through his rifle's powerful night-scope. He had to shake off home-front concerns.

Three kill shots later, judging by the shouts and then silence from outside, Deacon said, "Cover me. I wanna switch views."

"Hold up." Tristan had had the wherewithal to grab their night-vision helmets and now passed them out.

"Nice." Deacon fastened his in place.

Garrett typically would've thought to fetch those all-important accessories, but his head was back in Florida. If he didn't get his mind on the present game, he'd get them killed.

"Woof?" Deacon calling Garrett by the nickname he'd earned during BUD/S from being able to puke like a dog, then return to business, jolted him to his current reality. Lord willing, his mess with Eve would still be there when he got home. In this moment, nothing mattered more than all three of them staying alive and completing their assignment. "You got my back?"

"I'm on it."

The snow had lightened. Using his own "toy," Tristan said, "Got two heat signatures that ain't shaped like Bambi at four o'clock."

"On it." Two more shots later and Deacon had eliminated the threat.

Cockier than he should've been, Deacon inched farther from their cover to get a better view. Gunfire sent him back. "Shit, how many are there?"

"I'm seeing two additional heat signatures at six."

"Got 'em." Deacon took care of those, as well. "That's gotta be it..." He crept to the cave's mouth and so far, all was quiet.

Tristan followed with Garrett scanning all open space.

"I'm seeing one back at four o'clock, and—"

"Shit balls, that hurts." Tristan had been hit.

"Got him," Deacon said while Garrett assessed their friend's injury.

Tristan said, "Anyone else find it odd this sleepy mountain town has armed military scouts out on this hill in the middle of a freakin' blizzard?"

Garrett grunted. "Looks like we pretty much have our answer as to whether or not this burg is hiding a nuke party."

A couple more shots pinged off the rock walls.

"I'm going out," Deacon said. "These guys are pissing me off."

Garrett barked, "You're not going anywhere without cover."

"Both of you go," Tristan said. "I'm all right. He got my shoulder, but feels like it went clean through."

"You sure?" Garrett asked.

"Yeah." With his good arm, Tristan kept his heat imager steady. "Take out the shooter at eight, then your immediate path is clear. I say with the weather improving, let's forge ahead with our mission objectives, then get the hell out of Dodge."

Garrett couldn't have agreed more.

"DINA, I…" MOUTH DRY, knees rubbery, Eve wasn't sure what to say to Garrett's mom. She could lie and weave a story how the brochures were for a friend, but did she really want to go that route? She sharply exhaled, then tearfully admitted, "Yes, I'm pregnant with your son's baby, but I've already lost two pregnancies and our son, I don't have the strength to lose another and, and—" Now trembling, Eve clamped her hand over her mouth before embarrassing herself further.

"Come on." Dina wrapped her arm around Eve's slumped shoulders. To the receptionist, she said, "I'm sorry, but I have to go. I'll call to reschedule."

The receptionist nodded.

Thankfully, the waiting room was otherwise empty.

In Coral Ridge, ducks and green spaces outnumbered people and lucky for Eve, the medical park housing her doctor's office was no exception.

Through sun-dappled shade, Dina led her to a bench alongside a well-groomed lake. Once they were both seated and Eve had found tissues in her purse, Dina asked, "I have to know, were you ever planning on telling Garrett?"

"O-of course. Soon. I just didn't want him involved until I knew whether or not the pregnancy took. I really didn't see the need in getting anyone else upset if I lose this baby, too."

"The *need*," Dina said, "in sharing is as much good for you as our family. I refuse to believe this baby is anything but a blessing, and as such, however many months from now we'll welcome a baby boy or girl into our fold. Should the unthinkable occur, we'll deal with it—again, together. Eve, why would you want to tackle something so difficult by yourself? Especially when this whole town thinks of you as our own?"

"Th-that's just it." Eve pressed the tissue to her nose. "All my life I've had to keep up this perfect public persona, only I'm anything but perfect. I—I used to have my dad to help, but now, I feel so alone. And afraid. Like I just can't do it anymore."

Dina drew her into a hug and Eve dropped her guard enough to let her. Before Christmas, hugging a practical stranger would've been unthinkable, but now, at least with this warmhearted member of Garrett's clan, accepting Dina's comfort felt like the most natural thing in the world. Would she ever reach that emotional place with Garrett?

Once Eve had stopped sniffling, she backed to her own side of the bench. "I understand if you want to tell your mom or sister, but please let me tell Garrett in my own time."

"Of course," Dina said with a gracious nod, "if he's home by New Year's Eve, maybe then would be perfect for a big announcement?"

"That sounds amazing, but now I really should get to the office."

Dina tapped the pamphlets on the wood slats between them. "Wouldn't you rather share a nice, leisurely lunch? Carol and I already have reservations."

Forcing a smile, Eve said, "You know, a long lunch sounds like just what Dr. Seymour ordered."

EVE WORRIED A MEAL WITH a tight-knit duo like Dina and Carol would be painfully awkward, but talk flowed naturally while waiting for a table at a local teahouse, and Eve found herself enjoying the camaraderie of women who could've been her mother's contemporaries.

An hour later, with the table cleared of sandwiches and tiramisu for three on the way, Dina cleared her throat. "Carol." She took her sister's hand. "Though initially even I didn't know it, but it turns out we're here for a very special reason. Eve, the last thing I want is for you to feel as if I'm putting you on the spot, but would you like to tell Carol our fun news or shall I?"

"I will," Eve offered, actually anticipating sharing her good news.

"You two are scaring me." After a nervous laugh, Carol sipped her tea. "Enough of the lead-in. Out with it already."

Eve deeply inhaled, coaching herself on the probable certainty that everything with her baby would be okay. But would it? She'd already suffered two miscarriages. Fighting the knot lurking at the back of her throat, she said, "I'm pregnant, and the baby's Garrett's, and—"

Carol made a gasping sound and nearly knocked her chair over to jump up and give Eve a hug. "Sweetie, I know how much you value your privacy, but the whole town knows what you've been through with your pregnancies. I understand you wanting to be cautious."

"Thank you."

"I couldn't be happier," Dina said.

When Garrett's mom smoothed Eve's hair, it was the kind of maternal gesture she hadn't experienced since her own mother had died. Filled with an almost unbearable sweetness, she could've purred. She'd always enjoyed Garrett's mom, but this... What a surprise gift. "Thank you both for not being judgmental. Trust me, no one's more surprised than me, but I'm also happy. I want this baby. And I hope Garrett does, too."

GARRETT HAD ONLY BEEN BACK in Coral Ridge fifteen minutes, and while he probably should've at least stowed his gear at his mom's, then chatted with her over a turkey sandwich, all he really wanted to do was see Eve—or more specifically, see her so they could launch a fresh search for clues about their son. Knowing at three in the afternoon she'd still be at her office, he headed there.

After damn near getting himself and his friends

killed in North Korea, Garrett had to get his head back in SEAL mode. Best way to do that was to once and for all find his son, if at all possible establish a relationship with the little guy, then get back on base. As for Eve? He'd long since relegated her to his past, and that's where she needed to stay. He was selfishly glad his team hadn't made it back until after New Year's Eve. That way, he hadn't even been tempted to kiss her after the countdown.

During the long flight home, Tristan and Deacon had urged Garrett to do a thorough search of Hal's home, with his CO's blessing to take the time needed to complete his search, and Garrett vowed to look through every damned file in the mansion. If the old man had buried secrets, that's where they'd most likely be.

Not only did Garrett not find Eve at her office, but her assistant, Darcie, said she hadn't been in since that morning. Okay, odd, but probably a good thing. Lord knew, Eve needed rest.

He called her cell, but it went straight to voice mail. "Eve," he said, unsure what to even say, "it's, ah, Garrett. I'm back in town and need to see you. Call me."

His next stop was Eve's home.

Garrett always felt uncomfortable parking his Mustang in the circle drive. What if it dripped oil on the imported stone pavers? When he'd been a teen, a butler had appeared like magic before Garrett had even rung the bell. Now it took a few minutes for Juanita to appear.

"*Meester* Garrett!" The bosomy woman crushed him in a cinnamon-scented hug, but instead of her usual flamboyant hair, she was now dressed the part of a formal housekeeper.

"Whoa," he teased. "What happened to your fancy hair?"

She blushed. "I only wear it for Mr. Hal. Miss Eve be *soooo* glad you safe home." Eve had worried about him enough to share her concerns with Juanita? "She take nap. I wake her but have rolls in oven. You wake for me?"

Assuming the gist of the housekeeper's request was that he wake Eve while Juanita rescued her baked goods, Garrett agreed before heading up the imposing stairs.

At first, he went to the same room she'd had in high school, but that was a bust. It looked museum perfect, oddly frozen in time as if it were an exhibit used to show the life of a typical American girl—only even back then, Eve Barnesworth had been anything but typical. Garrett peeked in at least six other rooms with open doors, finally deducing she must be in the only one with a closed door.

He knocked.

"I'm up, Juanita," Eve called from inside.

Garrett eased the door open. "It's me. You decent?"

"You're back."

He entered to find her in the center of a canopied bed surrounded by movie magazines and three boxes of chocolates. The sun-flooded room had been done in yellow and cream. Eve was so pale, she blended with the sumptuous linens. Considering her long hair formed a bushy halo and she wore a Coral Ridge Football T-shirt over yoga pants, he couldn't help but ask, "Have you been drinking?"

"No." She made quick work of stacking her glossy reading material, gathering brown paper candy cups to toss in a bedside trash basket, then scooting off the bed to stand before him, looking as though she may have wanted to give him a hug, but wasn't sure if he'd accept. "When did you get home? Are you okay?"

"I'm good, but what's up with you being a lady of leisure? I stopped by your office and Darcie said she hadn't seen you all day."

She turned her back on him while tidying the bed. "My fainting spell scared me. I figured what could it hurt? You know, taking time just to *chill*."

Strange. The whole scene felt off. Completely out of character for the woman he knew who put her responsibilities toward those she employed far above her own needs.

He strode to an enormous arched, paned window, staring at acres of manicured lawn and gardens. Garrett had lost count of how many magazines the mansion and grounds had been featured in. Everything from *Architectural Digest* to *Southern Living*. The world saw this place as a living work of art. He saw it as the maze where he and Eve used to play tag when they were kids. The fountain where on particularly scorching summer days they'd waded in as teens. Back then, he never would've dreamed he and Eve's friendship could be shaken. Sure, he'd had his guy friends, but the bond he'd once shared with her had been extra special. "Remember when our third-grade class came here on a field trip to study your flowers?"

She'd joined him at the window. "My mom was still alive. I'm pretty sure she was crushing on the French gardener. Juanita, too."

He laughed. "Even as a kid, I remember that guy being awfully cool."

Now Eve was laughing. "Dad had a fit when Jacques started going to their parties. Said it was beneath them to socially mingle with staff."

"Yet, after your mom died, Juanita pretty much raised you, right?"

"Yes." Swallowing hard, looking as though a stiff breeze could topple her over, she shocked him by delivering that hug he'd earlier missed. "Which is why I'm glad you're home safe. Because up until—well, you know. You were always there for me, too. Thank you for that." Silent tears streamed down her cheeks. She made no move to wipe them away. "I had lunch with your mom and aunt Carol a few days ago. They're good women. They reminded me how much history you and I have shared—even way before what happened with our son."

"Okay, whoa." Leaning on the window, he faced her. "Something about you is *off*. And what the hell were you doing with my mom and aunt?"

She covered her face with her hands in what he feared was the start of a major sob fest, but then she lowered her hands and smiled. "Your mom's a nice person. So is Carol. I'll probably be seeing more of them in the future."

"Why?" Garrett didn't like the thought of his family getting chummy with Eve. Didn't like it one bit. His family was *his*. A safe place. Far from the chaos reigning whenever he and Eve shared a room.

"Does it matter? And anyway, why are you even here? It's not like you to show up unannounced."

"I want to launch a fresh search of this house for clues. I tried calling, but you weren't answering your cell."

"Oh." She had the good graces to redden. "I must've left it in my purse. Sorry."

"No apology necessary. You need a break, but seriously, what's going on with you? Since I've been gone, you've changed."

She opened her mouth, looking on the verge of telling him something, but then pressed her lips closed.

"Eve? Talk to me. What's going on?"

Chapter Twelve

Eve almost admitted to Garrett that the two of them were pregnant all over again, but couldn't do it. If she lost the baby, she couldn't bear the weight of him knowing she was a failure at the most basic act women were put on earth to do. Luckily, Garrett's mother had understood her reasoning. But the more Eve was with Garrett, the less she felt as if she truly knew him. The one thing she did know was that seeing him stroll through her bedroom door, healthy and handsome as ever despite wind-burned cheeks and overgrown hair, made her happier than she'd been in a long time.

"Don't ignore me," he pressed. "I'm not stupid, Eve. Does your sudden penchant for lounging in bed in the middle of the day have something to do with your fainting spell? You're not sick, are you? You don't have cancer?"

"No," she assured him. "I'm just mentally and physically exhausted and taking a break. End of story." Seated at her mirrored vanity to brush her hair, she asked, "You mentioned wanting to search for clues. Where do you want to start?"

"I guess your father's room. I know anything personal I want to hide, I stash in my closet."

"What are you hiding?" she couldn't resist asking. She'd put her hair in a side ponytail and felt lighter than she had in days. Blaming it on the congratulatory chocolates Dina had showered her with, Eve refused to believe her sudden inability to be serious had anything to do with her being happy about Garrett's return. "Girlie magazines? Piles of foreign loot?"

He sighed. "More like my passport and car-insurance papers. Anyway, would you be okay with us doing a serious search through Hal's stuff?"

"I'm all right with anything that helps find our son."

WHAT WAS WRONG WITH HIM?

Garrett was supposed to be engrossed in their search of Hal's obscenely large closet, but all he seemed capable of focusing on was the sight of Eve's derriere. Who knew yoga pants could be sexy as sin? Even worse, her T-shirt kept riding up, giving him glimpses of her abdomen and lower back.

"If you give me a boost—" Eve reached for a shelf above her head "—I think I can get that box."

"Sure." Though he could've easily grabbed it himself, Garrett took her up on her invitation, settling his hands low on her hips to lift her a couple feet. Her sweet floral smell was like nectar, making him only want her more.

"Got it." With the box in her arms, he lowered her down the length of him nice and slow, loving the feel of her softness against his strength. Once her feet hit the thick-padded carpet, he took longer than he should've to release her, but couldn't help himself. This light-hearted version of Eve made him doubt his resolve to stay away. Could her talk with his mother have had anything to do with Eve's change? If so, what could Dina have possibly said?

Eve sat on the floor, legs outstretched with the dust-covered box between them. "Whatever's in here, looks like it's been around awhile."

He sat next to her, leaning against custom teak cabinetry. Hal had a penchant for loud pants and they all now stared at Garrett. "So? What're you waiting for?"

"I feel like I'm going to get grounded."

He snorted. "I doubt you ever got so much as a time-out."

"Well…" She laughed. "I was trying to think up a witty comeback, but you're right. Aside from me getting pregnant, Daddy never had to worry too much about me."

"That's what I figured." He nudged her shoulder with his. "So open it."

She did and from his first glimpse, he wished she hadn't. More tears were imminent and he thought she'd already cried enough.

"I had no idea he kept these. This looks more like something Mom would've done."

Fingering the delicate pink ribbon binding report cards and glowing teacher reports, Garrett said, "She probably did. But then he took over when she was gone."

Sure enough, she began crying, dropping the stick-figure drawing of a mom and dad with a blond-haired angel in between them to dash for the bathroom.

She returned with a wad of tissues, drying her eyes and blowing her nose. "I've been so h-hard on him, but he was a wonderful father. I m-miss him so much."

"He stole our baby."

"B-but only because he thought he was helping us."

Garrett reached for the picture Eve dropped. In the process, he noticed part of the carpet was loose. He picked at it, only to get a shock when the whole section lifted out, revealing a floor safe.

Eve gasped.

"I take it you didn't know this was here?"

"No," she said, kneeling and fiddling with the combination knob.

"Any idea how to get inside?"

"Daddy was many things, but tech-savvy wasn't one. I'm running through birthdays and anniversaries." Two minutes later she had it open. "I'm honored my big day won."

"Whoa." Garrett reached past her to pull out bound stacks of hundreds. *Lots* of them. Next were more of Hal's manila files, followed by leather-boxed estate jewelry.

While Eve sat on her heels, oohing and ahhing over priceless necklaces, rings and earrings, Garrett was more interested in what Hal had considered worthy of filing, yet so sensitive in nature it'd had to be stored in a hidden safe.

It didn't take long to finally have tangible proof for what Garrett had suspected all along—Hal Barnesworth hadn't been a nice man. One folder netted careful logins of gifts he'd given women during multiple affairs. Column after column of Chanel purses. Another, a list of generous payoffs to various state officials for looking the other way for offenses ranging from forgiving three DWIs to encouraging zoning rulings to go in his favor to his most recent hiring of truckloads of illegal immigrants.

"I'll be damned..."

"What?"

Garrett flashed the contents of a particularly upsetting file. "Remember when we talked about my dad maybe having been influenced by Hal to stay out of Barnesworth business?"

She groaned.

"Around the time you left town, your dad made a hefty donation to the fire department—enough to buy five new trucks. Your dad wrote that he 'bribed Solomon to forget about my daughter and the baby by putting just the right squeeze on the budget. Talk—it goes down. Keep quiet—it goes way up. Threatened jobs, too, just to make sure he felt my request on an emotional level.'"

Eve's expression had changed from teary mourning to hardened anger. "Please tell me this is a bad dream…"

"Sorry." As much satisfaction as it'd given Garrett, learning the man the whole damn town touted as a hero had been the snake in the grass he'd always known him to be, he now felt that much more sad for Eve. She was the one left to deal with Hal's dirty legacy.

Flipping through the file listing Hal's extramarital affairs, she said, "I was only teasing about Mom and the French gardener. I always believed my parents had a fairy-tale marriage."

"Yeah, a dark fairy tale. Think she knew how many times Hal cheated?"

"She had to, which makes her life tragic." Talking more to herself, she dropped the file back into the safe. "Matt cheated on me. Even though by that point there was no love between us, it still hurt. Made me feel dirty. When I was a girl, one of my favorite things was sitting with Mom in one of the formal living rooms, sharing high tea, looking through her wedding album. Daddy was so handsome and she looked like a princess, complete with a diamond tiara holding her lace veil. Their wedding cake was seven layers tall and the parties lasted a long weekend. To this day, it's one of the largest wedding stories *Town and Country* has ever featured. When I think of fairy tales, my parents were the ultimate..." Teary gaze meeting his, she asked, "How could I have been so wrong?"

Never had Garrett wished more for a magic wand to whisk away Eve's pain. From losing her mom at such a tender age, to always having lived under Hal's thumb, she'd led a strange life. From the outside, she'd been envied, but even back when they'd dated, he'd sensed a deep sadness in her. All she'd ever wanted was to be honestly loved. She believed she'd had that in her father—and hell, Garrett didn't doubt the old bastard had loved her in his own warped way.

"If you don't mind—" he almost hated breaking the heavy silence "—I'm going to check out some of the women on your dad's list. Maybe one of them knows something about our son."

"They'd be too old."

"Still," he urged, "shouldn't we at least try?"

"I'm done. I really thought I could handle anything, but now I know I can't. Do what you want with this information, Garrett, but please, leave me out of it."

"You don't mean that." He gripped her shoulders, forcing her to face him. "I *know* finding our son means as much to you as it does me."

Instead of pushing him away, she sagged against

him, and he held her for all he was worth. *Yes, lean on me.* No matter what, he'd be there for her.

But for how long?

Even if he abandoned himself to the feelings he still had for her—had always had—that didn't mean she would, too. Beyond that, how was he supposed to continue his career in Coral Ridge? And Eve's heart was obviously stuck in their hometown.

"I'm not this weak person," she mumbled against his chest. "I never cry or feel defeated, yet lately, just facing each new day feels like an insurmountable goal."

"Give yourself a break." Hand beneath her chin, he said, "When I showed up this afternoon, you seemed to have everything under control. Don't let this crap about your dad bring you down."

"Easy for you to say." She left him to finger one of Hal's more colorful pair of golf pants. "Your dad was a hero. Mine was thought to be, but I'm now finding he was little better than an adulterer and common criminal. What am I supposed to do with that? What does his legacy say about me?"

"Nothing. With the exception of the illegal immigrants, all of it's in the past. Leave it there. It has nothing to do with you."

She nodded. "You really think contacting all those women on his list is worth a shot?"

Shrugging, he said, "Not like we have better leads to follow. In the meantime, let's take a walk…"

"You, GARRETT SOLOMON, are amazing." Eve tilted her head back, arms outstretched, turning in a slow circle while drinking in warm, winter sun. Garrett had taken her to their own secret garden, deep in the woods on her father's land. The white marble picnic pavilion was nestled alongside a lazy river, but a hurricane flood had carried off half the paver tiles and the place had been forgotten, only to be reclaimed by sinewy vines and rogue hibiscus. Ten-foot marble angels towered over each of the four corners and an arched marble pavilion took center stage, complete with wraparound circular benches. The trees now only allowed pieces of sun to enter in mysterious, slanted rays. Sweet, hidden blooms perfumed the air. "I'd forgotten about this place. You always used to bring me here whenever Sidney Calmount made me cry. You told me angels make everything better."

"Back then, they did." He sat on one of the marble balustrades, fingering the spot on a nearby cypress where they'd used bootlegged crab forks to carve their initials.

"With all due respect, our problems used to be a little easier."

"Did they?" Garrett asked. Far overhead a crow cawed. The sound was eerie amongst the already heavy hum of insects. "I came here when you first told me you were pregnant. And I came here again almost every day while you were gone. I used to close my eyes and pretend you came back to me. But you never did. And that made me sad. And angry. And until now, I was bitter and I didn't know who—if anyone—to trust."

"I'm sorry." Though she'd whispered her words, in this place they sounded inordinately loud. "You were the last person I ever meant to hurt."

"I know." He'd grabbed a stone, skipping it into the lazy river. "I shouldn't have even brought it up. Being here dredged up issues better left alone."

"But you brought me here to make me feel better."

He shrugged. "I'm guessing it didn't work?"

He flashed a sliver of a white-toothed smile that made her heart skip a beat. All over again Garrett became the little boy who at recess charged to her rescue. She adored him for that. And hated herself for ever causing him a moment's pain.

IN HER OFFICE THE NEXT morning, Eve couldn't shake a deep unease. After Garrett had been so sweet to walk with her to their old sanctuary, should she have returned the favor by accompanying him to talk with her father's mistresses? Was she a bad person for being more concerned about her own stress causing pregnancy complications than she was about finding the son she'd already lost?

A knock sounded on her office door, but before she'd even invited her guest in, Darcie had made herself at home. Comfy in the chair facing Eve's desk, she fanned herself. "Your man was looking good when he stopped by looking for you the other day."

"Garrett isn't mine." Eve didn't even bother looking up from the spreadsheet she'd been reviewing.

"Wouldn't know it by looking at him. Poor guy looks smitten. When I told him you weren't here, you'd have thought I told him steak ceased to exist."

"Steak?" Eve raised her eyebrows.

"I don't know." Darcie grinned. "Isn't that what military guys like him go for?"

Groaning, Eve covered her face with her hands. "Maybe. Here we already share one child, with another on the way, and I don't even know Garrett's favorite foods."

"Find out."

"It's not that simple." Eve returned to her spread-sheet.

"Sure it is. Ever think to ask?"

"That would mean I have to be around him."

Darcie laughed. "Like that's such a hardship?"

"Look." Eve struggled to find the right words. "I'll be first to admit the guy's gorgeous. And when we kiss…" Her cheeks flamed. "Well, in the chemistry department, everything still seems to work fine. But we're from different worlds. His strength makes me feel—" she waved her hands "—like some helpless baby bird. And you know that's not me. I'm not a damsel in distress, but whenever he's around, I feel like all I do is fall apart."

Darcie fiddled with the crystal dolphin Eve's dad had given her for her college graduation. He'd told her his dream for her was that she always felt confident and strong—capable of making great leaps and always going the distance. Just because she now knew him to be a liar, did that also mean he'd never been truthful with her? *Had* he wanted the best for her? Or had his beautiful words been more of the rhetoric he'd fed his constituents for the past forty years?

"That's why," Eve said, "I think it's best that even after, God willing, this baby is born, Garrett and I keep our distance."

"Okay, stop." As if dazed, Darcie shook her head. "You're making decisions you have no right to make on your own. Sooner, rather than later, Garrett deserves to know he's going to be a father. And did you ever stop to consider the reason you keep falling apart around Garrett is because deep down—" she patted her chest "—you *know* he's a man you can implicitly trust?"

GARRETT ROLLED ONTO HIS BACK and enjoyed the view. Even if Eve wasn't smiling as she approached the pool, that didn't make her less attractive in her pink skirt and jacket.

"Juanita said you were out here."

"I was early for our meeting and it's such a nice day…" He slicked water from his face and hair. "When Juanita offered to make me a sandwich poolside, I figured why not?"

"Did you bring swim trunks?"

He winked. "Wouldn't you like to know?"

"Garrett!" She covered her eyes with her hands. "What's Juanita going to think? What if any of her grandkids stop by?"

"I'll ask them to turn around while I get a towel."

"You're impossible."

"Join me," the devil made him ask. It'd been a lousy day, and as much as he hated to admit it, the mere sight of her had already made it a thousand times better. Just because he knew they'd never work long-term didn't mean he couldn't enjoy her company while he was in Coral Ridge. "Come on… It'll be fun."

For a moment, he could've sworn he'd caught a fleeting glimpse of longing—as if she wanted to do something outrageous like jump in with her clothes on or off, but wasn't quite sure how. "Thanks for the offer, but I really shouldn't."

Her answer annoyed the hell out of him. "Do you ever do things for pure, selfish pleasure?"

She sat at a poolside table. "I was raised believing it's not nice to be selfish."

He rolled his eyes. "Whatever."

Emerging from the pool, he didn't give a damn who saw him in his birthday suit—least of all, Prissy Missy. It wasn't the first time she'd seen him naked and if she weren't such a stick in the mud, it might not have been her last.

"Garrett!" She'd turned away, but not before getting a good long look at the view. "Seriously?"

He took his own sweet time toweling dry, then tugging on cargo shorts and a T-shirt.

Joining her at the table, he said, "Much as I hate admitting it, you were right about your father's harem. None of them knew a thing."

"Do you have to be crude?"

"Sorry. You think of a better term, I'll use it. Anyway, in between meetings, I got to thinking, maybe we've been going at this all wrong? Overthinking what's really a ridiculously simple solution."

Instead of seeming interested in his latest theory, she sat oddly slumped, hands curved over her abdomen.

"Stomach hurt?"

She shook her head, then straightened, striking a seemingly serene pose he knew she typically reserved for press conferences. "More like my heart. How long are you willing to go on like this? Chasing dead-end leads? Don't you have to get back to your job?"

"Sure, but this is our son, Eve. I'm not willing to just give up, and for the life of me, I can't understand how you are."

She sighed. "It's not that simple."

"Sure it is." He smacked the table. "Either you want

to find our boy or you don't. Period. Black and white. No shades of gray on this one."

Easy for you to say.

Upon her father's death, Eve's entire world had changed. Before she'd learned of her pregnancy, finding her and Garrett's stolen son had been her top priority, but with the fragile new life inside, she felt honor-bound to keep her stress level to a minimum. Constantly having her hopes raised only to then have them suffer crushing falls was getting too hard.

Mouth dry, pulse racing, she managed to say, "Please, tell me your latest plan."

His narrowed gaze brimmed with mistrust. "Sure you want to know?"

"If I didn't, I wouldn't have asked."

"So MUCH FOR THIS IDEA." Eve couldn't remember having ever seen Garrett look so defeated. His plan had been to launch a fresh approach to finding their son by checking out the one place eight-year-old boys would most likely be found—schools. They'd started at Thomas Howell Elementary, only to be brusquely told privacy laws didn't allow for any information regarding their students to be given. Three schools later, upon hearing virtually the same speech, Garrett had backed down.

"Sorry." With her hand on his forearm, Eve gave him a reassuring squeeze. "Though I can't say I'm surprised."

"I know." He sat behind the wheel of his car in a school lot. Sun beat through the windows, making the interior uncomfortably hot. "Are we wrong for not going to the cops? Or at least hiring a P.I.?"

Her stomach tightened at the idea. "I'm not ready for that. Maybe once we've exhausted all leads."

"Like we haven't already?" he asked with a narrowed stare. "Eve, I know the thought of us asking for outside help makes you uncomfortable, but if there's anything I've learned in the navy, it's that teamwork gets any job done."

"No." She'd been clear on the topic last time they'd discussed it. "You know how I feel about sharing our private business."

"This isn't *business,* Eve, but our child…" He'd softened his voice and turned to her. Every inch of her craved him, being held by him and reassured their search would turn out okay. Better than just okay. But for all of Garrett's strength, that didn't mean he was a superhero. He didn't have the power to make their son magically appear. Was he right? Was the search for their son bigger than them?

"Talk to me. What're you thinking?" Garrett asked.

She forced a breath. "Considering how many dead ends we've met on our own, you have my blessing to call for reinforcements—just promise you won't let this turn into a public spectacle."

"Promise." He not only met her gaze, but eased his fingers between hers. His touch soothed her like nothing else ever had. But why? Why didn't her body understand that he was never again going to be a permanent part of her life? Sure, because of their precious new child they'd always be connected, but as for more…

GARRETT FOUND STEWART Halsey, P.I., through a very high recommendation from Hal's attorney, Barry. There was nothing remarkable about the middle-aged guy—

from his receding hairline to his ample waistline to the cheap gray suit he wore with a beige tie hanging like a scarf from his neck. That said, the guy had a near-flawless record for completing the unconventional tasks he'd been given.

"Not gonna lie." Stewart sipped from a Mickey Mouse coffee mug. "This could be tricky." For the past hour, Garrett and Eve had shared every shred of information they'd gleaned, from Hal's mistress list to the mysterious redhead who Eve had confronted. "I like where you were headed in just personally checking out every eight-year-old in the state, but given privacy laws, as you found, that's a tad impractical."

"So what can we do?" Eve asked. "I—we—need to find our son."

"Agreed." Stewart steepled his hands, resting them beneath his chin. "My gut tells me the key to blowing this wide-open is the redhead."

"How do you think it went?" Garrett sat on the sofa in Hal's office, sifting through the never-ending mountain of files. Eve had parked at her dad's desk.

"Can't say I like the idea of Stewart following me, but if that redhead is still trailing me, I guess his theory makes sense. Unless we find some other lead here, at least Stewart will give us hope for progress."

"Yeah." He glanced up from mortgage papers on a rental building to find that Eve had leaned her head back and closed her eyes. He didn't think it possible for her to appear even more fragile and broken down, but she did. Dark circles had taken up seemingly permanent residence beneath her eyes and she'd lost even more weight. Looking at her, it occurred to him that he might want to shift gears now that they'd hired help. Getting Eve back in fighting condition could prove pivotal in how she ultimately handled whatever news Stewart found regarding their son. He faked a yawn. "I don't know about you, but I'm beat. That casserole Juanita made has me needing a nap—or hell, maybe we should just call it a night?"

"It's only eight," she noted after consulting her watch.

"Okay, we'll just break for a minisnooze. Please?"

"Go ahead." Nodding to the sofa, she said, "I'm not stopping you."

He asked, "What if I want company?"

He hadn't meant for the question to be in the least bit suggestive, but the way she narrowed her eyes told him she'd read it wrong. "Garrett…"

"Come on…" He stood, holding out his hand. "Your bed's enormous. Promise I'll keep to my own side."

"Truthfully," she said with a sad laugh, "I'm not even sure my legs will make it upstairs. As long as I'm in this chair, I should just barrel through the rest of these files."

"Or—" he scooped her like a rag doll into his arms "—you could nap with me."

"Garrett! Put me down!"

She wasn't even kind of a match for him, which she must've realized because she relaxed against him, tucking her face into the crook of his neck. For the duration of the trek upstairs, she unwittingly exhaled against sensitive skin. The heat pooling in his groin had him questioning his vow to remain a gentleman.

In her room, he rested her gently atop the comforter, then covered her with a soft throw he found folded at the foot of the bed.

When she sighed and smiled, he knew he'd made the right call. "This feels amazing."

He took off her shoes, carefully tucking the blanket around her feet. "Sure you're okay with company?"

She rolled over, patting the empty space alongside her.

Not needing a second invitation, he kicked off his shoes, then joined her. "You know, if you wanted to use me as a pillow, I'd be okay with it."

"Oh, you would?" she teased.

"Just sayin'…" He grinned as she sidled against him, resting her head in the crook of his shoulder while positioning her hand over his galloping heart.

"Mmm." She snuggled still closer. "Thank you. You were right. I do need a nap."

At least he'd accomplished his original goal of making Eve rest. Unfortunately for him he was suddenly wide-awake—and struggling with a below-the-belt issue her continued proximity only made worse.

EVE WOKE TO NOT ONLY find herself spooning with Garrett, but warmed by morning sun. While she should've forced herself out of bed and into the office, she relished the moment instead. The warmth of his hand unwittingly cupped their unborn child. What would it be like to wake every morning like this? Physically and emotionally secure? Bliss wouldn't begin doing justice to how amazing her life could be. But they'd already had their shot at happiness, and she'd blown it. Those kinds of second chances rarely came around again.

"Good morning." He nuzzled her neck. "Guess we brought new meaning to falling asleep on the job?"

"Yeah." Covering his hand with her own, she asked,

"Is it wrong a part of me would like nothing more than to hide out like this forever?"

"No, but—" he kissed the back of her head "—that would mean we may never find our son. Or, worse yet, eat Juanita's pancakes."

Unable to keep from laughing, she rolled over to give him a swat. "You're thinking of food at a time like this?"

He patted her behind. "Just doing my part to help fatten you up. I like a woman with a little meat on her bones."

On the surface, his statement read innocently enough, but dig a fraction deeper and Eve couldn't keep from wondering what he'd really meant. Was he starting to think of her in terms of being *his woman?* Would she like that? Or would that only further complicate her life?

"I have plenty of meat, thank you very much." With the mood broken, she slid off the bed. "Go ahead and ask Juanita for whatever you want for breakfast. I'm going to grab a quick shower."

"Will do." Still in bed, he stretched. "Nervous about today?"

"A little," she admitted. "But mostly about what we do if the infamous redhead doesn't show." With Stewart, they'd decided to use Eve as bait. On the off chance the woman showed up again, Eve would make herself as available as possible.

"If she doesn't, we'll just move on to plan B."

Swallowing hard and willing herself not to cry, Eve nodded. Yet again, Garrett had proved to be the strong one between the two of them. But like Darcie had pointed out, was that so bad? Why was it so hard for Eve to not only let him take the lead, but enjoy it?

Melting her with his smile, he assured her, "We *will* find our son."

Chapter Thirteen

It took eleven days for the redhead to surface.

While Eve shopped or ran errands, Garrett had been riding along with Stewart, keeping an eye out for the woman should she appear again. Once she did, Stewart made a few calls to run her plates and within ten minutes had *Dawn Henry's* street address in Harbor View, which was a good thirty miles south. They'd also learned she was married and had an eight-year-old son—Boyd. Coincidence? Garrett prayed not.

An hour later, Garrett and Eve sat in his car a few houses down from the home where it was possible their son lived. Stewart had offered to go with them in case the meeting went dicey, but Garrett and Eve agreed they'd rather initially meet with the woman on their own.

"What're you thinking?" he asked Eve.

"Part of me hopes more than anything this is it—we finally found our son. But if he's happy and leading a wonderful life, then what? It's not like we can just take him. I mean, legally, we probably eventually could, but morally, if he's happy, it would be reprehensible. On the flip side, one day, he will eventually need to know he has birth parents out there who would like nothing more than to share a meaningful relationship with him."

"Yeah..." Garrett sighed. "That's about the gist of what I'm thinking, too. So now what? School doesn't get out for hours. There's a car in the drive. Do we just march up to the door and ring the bell?"

"I don't know." Eve's voice sounded thin.

"Hey." He made a stab at tenderness, taking her hand. "Everything's going to be all right. Yeah, I'd be lying if I said a selfish part of me didn't want to find him in a lovingly run orphanage where we'd charge in to rescue him and shower him with toys, but in the grand scheme of things, the current scenario of him already being part of a happy family is probably best." He gave her fingers a squeeze. "Lord knows, we're in no shape to give the kid a stable home, right?"

Eyes watering, she nodded.

"Okay, so let's— Whoa. See that?"

The front door on the immaculately groomed ranch-style home opened and out walked a redhead dressed in warm-ups, carrying an iPod. Once clear of the drive, she jogged in their direction.

Hands over her mouth, Eve said, "Th-that's her."

"Who?"

"Tina Northridge—or, Dawn Henry—whoever she really is. I didn't connect it before, but that's her car parked in front of the house."

Garrett climbed out of his Mustang.

"What're you doing?" Eve asked in a loud whisper.

"What do you think? Asking her flat out if she has our son."

Garrett didn't want to startle the woman, but in the same respect, he needed answers only she could give.

Approaching her with his hands in his pockets, he called from a good thirty feet, "Tina Northridge? Or is it really, Dawn Henry?"

She stopped and paled. Glancing toward her house as if contemplating a charge in that direction, she then spotted Eve exiting the car and burst into tears. "I—I'm sorry. I—I never would've taken him had I known..."

Eve asked, "You're admitting you have our son?"

Gaze darting, the woman said, "C-can we do this inside? I'd prefer the neighbors not see."

For Eve, surreal didn't begin to describe the feeling of sitting in Dawn Henry's neat-as-a-pin living room, surrounded by photos of a little boy who had Garrett's striking gray eyes. After all their searching, they'd finally found their son.

"Can I get either of you something to eat or drink?"

"No, thank you." Deeply ingrained manners were the only thing keeping Eve from a verbal assault. "If you wouldn't mind, please just let us know how you came to have our son."

The woman cleared her throat. "I—I used to be your father's secretary."

"No." Eve shook her head. "Gladys has been—was—his secretary for years. She's practically family."

Seated ramrod straight in a side chair, hands pressed on her knees, Dawn forced a breath. "Remember when Gladys had back surgery? I filled in for her. Personally, it was a horrible time. My husband, Steve, and I were desperate for a baby, but nothing worked. Our third stab at in vitro had just failed and Steve and I were hardly speaking. Your father was so kind and work became my haven. One thing led to another and…" She flopped her hands.

"Yeah, yeah, we get it." Garrett folded his arms.

Seated beside him on a sofa, Eve felt his tension through the rigidity of his pose.

"Anyway, Hal and I—well, we had I guess what you'd call a fling. It didn't mean anything. Just two lonely people passing time. Steve traveled a lot and without children, I…" She stood, plucking a photo of their son from the mantel, tracing his features. "Look, I never stopped loving my husband, and Hal knew Steve was the love of my life. Hal also knew I couldn't have my own children and when he offered me your baby, he told me I would be doing you two a huge favor. Helping you fix a 'problem.' My best friend is Coral Ridge's librarian and when she told me what you two were doing, launching a search to find your son, I wanted to tell you. That's why I've been following you, Eve. It's become an obsession, but I haven't been able to admit the truth. Never, for one second, would Steve and I have taken your son if we'd known Hal told you—" She stopped as if her love for Boyd was so great she couldn't even bear contemplating his death. "Please…" She hugged the photo. "At least for the time being, I'm begging you to keep this between us. I know you have every legal right to take back your son, but until he's a little older, I don't see the need to destroy his happiness. Steve and I have never gotten along better and he didn't know about my affair with Hal."

Garrett scoffed. "He wasn't curious how you suddenly ended up with a baby?"

"Hal spoke to him, told him we'd be doing all of you a huge favor. Eve, your father begged us for discretion, set up a generous trust for Boyd's future education and that was that. Steve and I both believed we'd not only had our prayers answered, but in turn, answered yours."

Eve glanced at Garrett to find his lips pressed tight and hands fisted. What was going through his head? Never had she wished they were closer. That she knew him enough to read his every thought just from his body language.

"Please." Dawn was again crying. "I'm begging you to at least temporarily leave everything alone. Your son is happy and healthy and—"

Garrett said, "I need to meet him." Turning to her, he said, "Eve, I suspect you feel the same?"

She nodded.

"I don't give a damn what you tell your husband." Garrett's voice lacked a trace of compassion. "I get that if your story's on the up-and-up, just like us, you also fell victim to Hal's lies. But that doesn't change the fact that you essentially stole our son. So in exchange for our current silence, I'm gonna need you to arrange a party or whatever scenario you choose, but within the next couple days, I *have* to talk to my son."

"D-do you feel the same?" Dawn asked Eve.

"Yes." Eve's throat was tight as Garrett and Dawn exchanged numbers, and she was profoundly grateful to him for yet again tackling a situation she couldn't.

"COULD YOU USE A DRINK?" Garrett asked Eve on the short trek back to her home.

"Love one, but my stomach's too upset."

"Mind tagging along with me to Schmitty's? Honestly, I'm not up to being alone." Admitting his vulnerability had never been a strong suit, but this was one time when his need for comfort and mutual understanding far outweighed pride.

He glanced her way to find her struggling for an answer and tightened his grip on the wheel. "Dammit, Eve, has whatever friendship we had dwindled to the point you can't even bear sitting across a table from me?"

"It's not that," she assured him. "I just can't handle a bar right now. Anywhere else will be fine. If you want, Juanita's visiting Miami relatives, so we can hang out at my house. Maybe go for a swim—if you promise to wear trunks." When she smiled briefly, curving her delicate hand over his forearm, he regretted snapping. Why was everything regarding her such a big deal? Ordinarily, he had the patience of a saint, but with Eve he was always on guard. She made him crazy—not in a good way.

While he grilled steaks by the pool, she made a salad and asparagus. They eventually met up, seated across from each other at one of the poolside tables, neither saying a word. The night was balmy without a breath of wind. Somewhere on the vast estate, a whip-poor-will sang a lonely song.

"This is good." He finally broke the silence. "Thanks."

"Thank you. My steak's perfect."

"We ever going to talk about this afternoon?" He'd hoped to broach the topic of their son in a more organic way, but had tired of waiting. Whether she needed to, or not, he had to get things off his chest.

"I'd like to—" she forked a bite of salad "—but what is there to say? Pretty much the whole thing played out just like we figured. Part of me is angry—like I want to storm over there right now and take what's rightfully ours. But this is a boy we're talking about, not a necklace or stolen car."

"Yeah," he agreed, dredging a piece of steak through some A.1. sauce. "Even worse, any contact we do manage to make is going to have to be done as family friends. Right off the bat, if we so much as hint at the fact we're Boyd's true parents, the poor kid's going to freak. Then any chance we might've had at getting to know him slowly is shot."

"Right. So, where we're concerned, it's a lose-lose scenario."

Garrett growled. "Don't say stuff like that. SEALs don't lose."

"Hate to be the bearer of bad news, but you're a man first, Garrett. And in this case, we've both lost twice— at least for the time being. As for what our future with Boyd may hold, let's hope for the best."

At the moment, *the best* didn't seem anywhere near good enough, which only frustrated Garrett all the more. "Ever feel like your dad's still pulling our strings from beyond the grave?"

"Every day..." She stared beyond the pool, to where a light fog hovered over grass so flawless it didn't look real. What was the point? How many thousands had Hal thrown away each year on his lawn? Just one more issue he and Eve's father hadn't seen eye to eye on.

"What're we going to do?" Garrett wasn't accustomed to feeling adrift. As if every move he made toward their son could be a land mine.

"Wait for a call."

"I don't like waiting."

"I know." When she smiled, her sweet, simple beauty stole his breath away. More than anything, he wanted to take her into his arms, but considering he'd soon be leaving, the last thing either of them needed was one more action clouding where they stood. "Wanna take that swim?"

He couldn't resist teasing, "Do I have to wear a suit?"

She pitched her napkin at him, which he easily dodged.

"There are plenty in the guesthouse. Help me clear the table and then we'll change and meet back up."

"Since when are you such a demanding wench?"

Laughing while grabbing a plate, she said, "Feels good for a change. I've been such a wet noodle lately. Emotionally wobbling. For me, at least knowing where our son is and that he's safe, happy and healthy feels better than the wondering."

Trailing her into the kitchen, Garrett wished he could be as at peace with their situation. Not that she was any happier than he was, but at least she was capable of putting words to her feelings.

He made it in the pool before she did, which afforded him a painfully good view of Eve striding toward him in a white bikini. Though thinner than he'd like, she still had curves in all the right places. And damn if her breasts didn't seem bigger—never a bad thing.

"I already grabbed a couple towels." He nodded toward a chaise near the steps.

"Thanks." She kicked off her sandals, groaning with pleasure when she stepped in to find the water bathtub warm. The pool lights must've been set on a timer as they came on, surrounding Eve in an ethereal blue glow. "The water's perfect."

"I'd hate to see your utility bills."

She winced. "You know, this is embarrassing to

admit, but I've never even seen the figures for what it takes to maintain this place. Guess I should probably think of selling."

He floated on his back. "You need the money?"

"I don't think so, but this place is a little much for two people. I keep telling Juanita to invite her family for visits, but she tells me, 'Meester Hal, he no like row-dee keedz in pool.'"

Laughing, Garrett said, "Guess she's not the only one having a tough time remembering he's gone?"

"Yeah…" Eyes watering, Eve swooshed the water in front of her, lips pressed tight as if fighting the need to cry. "I don't know what's wrong with me. One minute I'm okay, then the enormity of missing him weighs me down like one of those lead X-ray aprons they put on you at the dentist. I'm so mad at him, but I can't stop loving him. It doesn't make sense."

"Doesn't have to." Should he go to her? Though he knew being anywhere near her was a bad idea, he gravitated closer. "When I lost Dad, there were times I didn't think I'd survive it. Like I couldn't catch my breath. To this day, I'll have something quirky happen and think, I need to call Dad. Everyone says, he's always here. You can talk to him anytime you like, but…" He shrugged. "It just isn't the same."

She wiped tears and nodded. "Does a part of you feel like we've essentially been told our son died all over again, too?"

Honestly, yes. But he hadn't wanted to go there. Not with her still so sensitive over losing Hal.

Not giving a damn what he *should* do, Garrett flowed through the water to her, wrapping her snug against him. She fit just right, just as she always had. Years faded until holding her felt like a natural extension of himself. As much as he'd tried compartmentalizing her away, she'd never left his soul. His time with her was forever etched inside like an image burned into a TV screen. Ghostly. There, but not really. Not in a tangible, meaningful way.

He drew back to look at her, brushing tears from her cheeks with the pads of his thumbs. Did she have any idea how much she meant to him? Would she even care?

He gravitated closer and closer until he kissed her without reason. There were some things in life that couldn't be labeled and his physical attraction for her certainly fit that bill.

Warm water lapping ultrasensitized skin, he lifted her, urging her legs around him as he walked backward into the deep, not wanting her to catch a chill. As night fell around them, he fell deeper under her spell. Her soft mews told him he wasn't the only one overtaken by raw physical need.

He removed her top, only to leave it bobbing alongside them. The weight of her breasts felt heavy and good in his hands—even better mounded against his chest when he kissed her again.

Off came his trunks.

The bottom to her string bikini was all too easily undone.

With her legs and arms back around him, entering her came as natural as breathing. She clung to him, thrusting to meet him, nipping his ear.

He lasted just long enough to feel a subtle change inside her, just long enough to hold her close as she arched her head back and moaned.

Finished, guilt should've consumed him, but he refused to feel anything other than hard-won pleasure. Together, they'd been to hell and back. Who's to say they weren't entitled to a sliver of heaven?

"AGAIN? AND IN THE POOL?" Darcie made quite a show of fanning herself on the sofa in Eve's office. "My, my, aren't we becoming quite the little hussy?"

"Oh, stop." Eve didn't look up from her report. "You're making me regret even telling you."

"I'm just teasing. So what happened after? Any wild love admissions or at least a marriage proposal?"

"Would you please be serious?" Eve begged.

"I am." Darcie bit into the banana she'd brought with her. The smell made Eve the tiniest bit nauseous. The further along in her pregnancy she grew, the more sensitive her nose became. "He's gorgeous, smart, funny, you're having his baby—why wouldn't you marry him?"

"It's complicated." Abandoning her pencil, Eve pressed the heels of her hands to her forehead. "Not only is there soon-to-be physical distance between us, but emotionally, we're not even on the same page. He's all strong and tough and gung ho. I'm a marshmallow. Around a campfire, he'd be the stick that stabs through me, then douses me in fire."

Rolling her eyes, Darcie asked, "When have you, Princess Eve, ever been camping?"

"You know what I mean. In layman's terms, we're not good for each other. Oil and water."

"But sometimes opposites can be good together. Spicy salsa chased with an ice-cold margarita."

Eve sighed, flipping through a trade magazine. "You're missing my point. And anyway, if it hadn't been for us finally finding our son, we wouldn't have even been together. Trust me, it was strictly a one-time thing."

Wrinkling her nose, Darcie asked, "Isn't that what you said the last time?"

ON HIS WAY TO PICK UP EVE, Garrett called Tristan. Used to be he'd have talked over woman issues with Deacon, but now that his old pal was happily married, he'd turned a little too Pollyanna for Garrett's tastes. Ask him, all that domestication had stolen Deacon's objectivity.

After having been debriefed on Garrett's most recent life events, Tristan whistled. "You're in a little too deep down there for my liking. Time to extract yourself ASAP."

"See? That's what I think, too. The more I'm with Eve, the more I want to be with her, but there's the whole distance thing, and I honestly can't say I've ever gotten over the way she hurt me so bad before. I like her, but I don't trust her. What kind of foundation is that?"

"None at all, my friend. In the short term, your son is a lost cause. Don't let yourself fall victim, too. We need you back here, man."

Garrett agreed to return to base as early as possible, but upon ending the call was consumed with guilt. Last night, he and Eve had shared a remarkable moment in time. But if pressed, he had to concede that one moment didn't make for more. In all fairness to himself, Eve had once hurt him to an unfathomable degree. It'd taken him years to recover and he still couldn't sustain a decent relationship. She'd taught him at an early age not to trust, and he carried that lesson with him to this day.

But, his conscience had to point out, had she been responsible for his pain or her father?

He pulled up to the home that'd been in Eve's family practically since Florida had gained statehood. The place was as imposing as the men who'd built it and once lived within.

Garrett wasn't a man who easily caved under intimidation, but this house represented everything he wasn't. If Eve was looking for monetary power, Garrett would never be her man. If she wanted integrity, a man who never gave up, he'd be the perfect guy for her, but judging by the ease with which she'd not only forgotten him, but went on with her life to the tune of marrying another man? Well, that proved how low Garrett rated.

Just as he was climbing from his car, Eve bounded out the front door, cheeks flushed as if she'd been rushing. As usual, her simple grace knocked the breath from him and derailed his resolve to forever free himself from her unwitting hold. With her long hair streaming down her back and pale yellow dress clinging to her curves, his mouth went dry and his pulse raced.

Before he could help her with the passenger door, she opened it herself. "Hope I didn't keep you waiting."

"Not at all," he said from back behind the wheel. "Ready for this?"

She shook her head. "How was telling your mom?"

He started the car. "As awkward as you might think. She wanted to tag along—*bad*."

"Did you explain to her how rough this is going to be even for us?"

"Sure." he pulled out of the drive and onto the street. "But once Mom gets hold of something, she doesn't let go. You've been fortunate not to see that side of her."

Eve coughed before turning on the AC and pointing it toward her still-flushed face.

"You all right?"

"Fine."

The knot in Garrett's gut told him nothing would ever again be truly fine.

Chapter Fourteen

Eve had learned all too well how determined Dina could be when it came to having her way. The woman had been relentless in her gentle urging to tell Garrett about the pregnancy, but the timing hadn't seemed right.

Every light in the Henry home seemed to be on, and judging by the muted sounds of laughter and silverware clinking from the backyard, the soccer-club party Dawn had offered to host was in full swing. The base from pop music pulsed through uncomfortably muggy night air.

"Still blows my mind," Garrett said on the endless walk from where they'd parked on the street to the house's front steps, "how Dawn's husband only knows they adopted their son from us, but he's clueless about the affair."

"Hal strikes again..."

"No kidding." He rang the bell. "Sure you're up for this?"

"Of course. Why wouldn't I be?"

He shrugged. "No specific reason, I guess. You've seemed distracted for a while."

"I'm good." She forced a smile. How long had she dreamed of having a child, and now she had one and another coming? In a weird way, Eve identified with

Dawn. She knew all too well the empty heartache stemming from being unable to conceive. The fact that she had so easily with Garrett for a second time hadn't escaped her notice. Did the man have super SEAL sperm?

The silly question brought much-needed levity to the impossibly difficult night.

"What's so funny?" Garrett rang the bell again.

Nothing I can tell you.

Eve was saved from answering by Dawn opening the door. "Hi, come in. Steve knows who you are, but I hope you don't mind, Eve, but since you're practically Coral Ridge royalty, I told everyone else Barnesworth Industries is presenting the soccer team with an award. It's just a silly certificate. I've already printed it out. All you have to do is hand it to the team captain."

"That sounds good." Eve appreciated Garrett's hand warming the small of her back, securely guiding her through the maze of unfamiliar faces. How could she have lived in the town practically her whole life, yet there were still so many people she'd never before seen? Worse yet, it seemed everyone aside from Boyd wanted to talk. Share their condolences or memories of her father.

"This is nuts," Garrett said in her ear once they'd stolen a moment alone. His warm breath made her shiver. "I've only caught two glimpses of Boyd all night."

"I know. Do you want this?" She nodded to her plate. "I'm too nervous to eat."

He took her remaining chopped brisket, slaw and deviled eggs. "Hell, I'm too nervous to do anything but eat."

"I suppose, in a way, it's good we're obviously such outsiders."

"How so?" He'd already cleared half the plate.

"It's certainly squelched any lingering delusions I might've had about Boyd suddenly recognizing us, running up to us with his arms outstretched for a Hollywood-style epic hug."

Shaking his head, Garrett's smile was bittersweet. "Gotta admit, I had the same thought. And since we're already feeling like crashers at our own party, can I just say I hate the name Boyd. Who does that to a kid?"

"Me, too. It's horrible." On autopilot, she used her napkin to wipe a smudge of barbecue sauce from Garrett's chin.

"Thanks."

"You're welcome." He'd always been passionate about his food. How many times when they'd been in the high-school cafeteria had Eve adoringly cleaned him? She used to feel proprietary where he was concerned. As if he'd always belong to her and only her. Being around him again had ignited so many old instinctive feelings where he was concerned, but he'd soon be leaving and by night's end, the whole reason behind Garrett even still being in town would be gone. The search for their son would've come full circle in a poignant ending neither had wanted but feared from the start.

The night wound on with more small talk than Eve had patience for. Her whole life, she'd been schooled in the art of talking while essentially saying nothing at all. Whether happy about it or not, she could go on for hours more, but what was the point? When would she finally speak with the one little boy who mattered?

When the time came for Eve to present her pretend

award, she'd added a large check from her personal account.

Upon accepting the money, the team captain asked, "Is this real? I've never seen that many zeros in my life!"

The adults clapped and whistled and all was well except in Eve's lonely heart. Garrett still stood beside her, but she knew that, too, would soon come to an end. Eventually Dawn brought Boyd to Eve, telling the boy to thank her.

"Thanks, Ms. Barnesworth," he said with an achingly formal handshake. "Now, we can go to nationals."

"That sounds fun." Eve knelt to his eye level. "Y-you all must be pretty good?"

"Yeah! Last year we were undefeated. We haven't started this year, but pretty soon."

"H-how exciting." Eve hadn't wanted to release her son's hand. *Her son.*

Garrett asked, "What position do you play?"

"Goalie!"

"Wow. I'm impressed. Ever get hurt?"

"Nah." Boyd looked to his mom. "Have I been nice long enough? Can I go back to my tree house?"

Tears lodged in Eve's throat, clawing like barbed wire.

She thought she'd previously known pain, but nothing could've prepared her for this—for being an unwanted duty in her own son's life.

To Dawn, Eve managed to say, "Thank you. He's, um, obviously a happy child. Garrett…" She locked gazes with him, silently begging for him to help free them both from this hellish situation.

Garrett said, "We should get going."

"You're welcome to stay." Dawn's gaze followed Boyd across the yard. "Steve's making a fire for s'mores."

"Thanks, but we can't." *I can't. This is too hard.*

Dawn crushed her in a hug. "Promise, I'll tell Boyd you're his birth parents soon. Just let me find the right time. Steve and I knew we'd eventually tell him he's adopted once he gets older, but now that you're both in the picture, we'll move up our schedule."

"We'd appreciate it," Eve said.

"Until then," Dawn reassured them, "Steve and I will look for more opportunities to ease you into Boyd's life. We want him to see that far from this being upsetting for him, all it really amounts to is him having more people in his life who love and care about him." Her words might've been brave, but her eyes shone with emotion.

"Thank you. We'll be in touch." Eve was never more relieved than when Garrett slipped his arm about her waist, guiding her toward the front door.

She quietly sobbed the whole ride home, and when she asked Garrett to come in, he politely declined.

Hands in his pockets as he stood beside her at her front door, he said, "Before tonight, I thought for Mom I might stick around a few more days, but I can't. To-night—this whole fruitless search has been too hard. I mean, yeah, we'll eventually be part of Boyd's life, but it's not going to be the reunion I'd prayed for. I've got to get back to something real, you know? I'm heading back to base first thing in the morning."

More tears welled in a tearful, never-ending loop. *Damn you, Garrett Solomon. What the two of us share is real. For whatever reason, you just don't want to see.* But then in all fairness, did she? They were different in so many ways. It'd be impossible to erase their past to start over anew.

When he wrapped his arms around her, yet again lending his support, Eve clung to him for dear life. She wasn't sure how, but in the time since he'd been back to Coral Ridge, he'd once again become her life. For all of her brave thoughts just moments ago, she now shamefully begged, "Please don't go."

"You'll be fine," he assured her, stroking her back, kissing the top of her head. "Tonight cost both of us. It was awful letting our son go. But tomorrow, you'll see that just like leaving him with his family was the right thing, so is my departure."

"What if it wasn't? What if I'm having second thoughts about not telling Boyd we're his parents right now? Not only that, what if I need you?" she confessed, and truthfully had only just wholly realized. How would she make it through her pregnancy without him? Let alone raising their child on her own?

"If Dawn still hasn't told him, we'll revisit the idea of telling Boyd he's really our son in a couple months. As for you needing me? No, you don't." Releasing their hug only to grip her upper arms, he said, "Eve Barnesworth, you are one of the smartest, toughest women I know. Sure, lately, things have been rough, but that'll change. Every day you're getting stronger and you've got the good parts of your father in you. Hell, maybe one day you'll even run for mayor?"

She laughed through a fresh sob. "That's the last thing I want." But what did she want? *To be Garrett's wife?* In light of his cruelly polite exit, she'd essentially been nothing more to him than a holiday diversion. "Would you stay if I told you I was pregnant?"

For never-ending seconds, he searched her face. "Are you?"

Tell him! her conscience screamed, but why, logic questioned. He obviously didn't want to be with her long-term. Was she prepared to spend the rest of her life clinging to a man who didn't see her as part of his future? Had grief for her father and stolen son pushed her to that pathetic state? No.

"Eve? Are you or are you not pregnant with my child?"

Raising her chin, demanding her tears once and for all stop, Eve summoned every trace of her Barnesworth strength. "Sorry. I'm not sure why I even asked the question. Our meeting with Boyd was truly awful and I'm not myself."

"Sure. I understand." He noticeably exhaled. Relieved he wasn't going to be a father? She wanted so badly to tell him everything, but this realization hurt worse than the combined pain of what she'd already been through. She didn't know where to start in defining what she felt for him, but she knew he didn't want to be a part of her life again, and that made her feel vulnerable. Naked to her core. "All right, then, so I guess this is it? Keep me posted on any more meetings you get with Boyd, then we'll set something up for us to see him together when I'm in for Easter?"

"Sure. Sounds perfect."

"Great." He flashed her the smile that never failed to stir butterflies in her stomach. "If that meeting's as tough as tonight, we'll share a drink, too."

Not likely. By then she'd be big as a house.

"Okay," she said with a wobbly nod. "That'll be nice."

Nice and torturous.

"Great." He tossed his keys up and down on his palm. "I'll call to set up a time."

WOULD YOU STAY IF I TOLD you I was pregnant?

Packing his gear at 5:00 a.m., Garrett couldn't get Eve's question from his mind. Would he? Stay? Would he have honestly been prepared to give up the only part of his life that made sense? Being a SEAL wasn't just a job. In the navy, he'd figured out how to once again feel whole without her. He could do good for others, while at the same time forgetting the damage done to him—both tasks he'd accomplished all too well up until recently.

His mind's eye returned to their time in the pool. To the feel of losing himself inside her—not just how he'd physically felt, but the emotional attraction he feared he'd always have for her. And why fear that? Because it got him nowhere he needed to be. Someday, he'd very much like to be a father. Settle down with a good woman who made him whole. But that woman wasn't Eve. Could never be Eve. Too much had transpired between them.

"I made you sandwiches and cookies and a thermos of coffee." Dina stood teary-eyed at his bedroom door, holding a grocery bag.

"Thanks, Mom." He pulled her into a hug. "You didn't have to do that."

"I know," she sniffed, "but I have to do something. Every time you leave it gets harder."

"Mom, I'll be fine. Promise."

That only brought more tears. "Don't make promises you can't keep. Your dad promised to be home early the day he died. We were supposed to play bridge at the Andersons' that night."

"Mom…" Garrett knew his job was dangerous, but being a SEAL was the only job he knew.

"You never told me how last night went. Did little Boyd seem to sense any connection with you and Eve?"

Back to shoving socks in his gunnysack, Garrett laughed. "The kid was in his own world—which I get. It was hard, though. Dawn and Steve promised to tell him about his biological family soon. Until then, we'll get to know him as family friends."

Swallowing hard, she nodded. "How did you and Eve end things?"

"All right, I guess. It was a little awkward, but that's to be expected." He hefted the bag over his left shoulder.

"She didn't have anything special to tell you?"

"Not that I can remember."

"Hmm." She led the way out of his room.

"Give me one more hug, then I've gotta hit the road." Holding his mom felt extra sweet. He'd enjoyed his time with her. He used to worry about her being on her own, but he now knew she'd grown a new life brimming with good friends.

"I love you." She kissed his cheek at the front door. It was still dark outside and light fog made streetlights fuzzy.

"Love you, too, Mom." He gave her another hug. "Please stop crying. I'll be home soon."

She nodded before waving him on his way.

WHEN EVE PASSED DARCIE'S DESK, her supposed friend said, "You look like death warmed over."

Eve gave her a dark glare. "Trust me, I know. Could you do me a huge favor and cancel my meetings?"

"You only have two. The Rodgers acquisition and a legal update for progress on the immigration issues. Want me to sit in for you and take notes?"

"Perfect. I owe you." In her office, Eve tossed the light sweater she'd worn with her fawn-colored blouse and pencil skirt over the nearest chair. Her eyes were swollen and stinging from crying and her feet had ballooned from too much standing in heels the night before. The moment she settled into her desk chair, she kicked off her black pumps.

"So?" Darcie had shut the door and now occupied a guest chair. "How was your meeting with Boyd? Love at first sight?"

"Not exactly." Eve started her computer. "After what couldn't have amounted to more than a minute's worth of meaningless conversation, he dashed off on his merry way. Garrett and I made our departure, and that was that. The Henrys promised we'll see more of him soon, but after all we've been through to find Boyd, a promise doesn't seem like enough. I understand, but I want my son. Now."

"Oh, Eve…" Her friend rounded the desk for a sideways hug. "I'm so sorry."

"Wait, it gets better. Garrett dropped me at the house and as usual, I couldn't stop crying, so in a move only I'm dumb enough to make, I asked if I were pregnant, if he would stay, then—"

"What? You told him you love him and about the baby?"

"Thank God, I didn't go that far. Almost, but not quite—which is good because when he seemed relieved there wasn't a baby in our future, my insides felt shredded. With everything in me, I finally realized how much he's come to mean, only it's too late for us. I've made a mess of anything special we once shared and there's no fixing it. And now that he's gone—"

"Wait—" Perched on the edge of Eve's desk, Darcie asked, "Gone, as in back-to-Virginia Beach gone?"

Eve nodded.

Darcie whistled. "No wonder you're freaking inside."

"Actually, now that the whole ugly scene is over, I'm vowing to be better. Stronger than I've felt since Dad… well, you know."

Eve started answering an email, but then her traitorous emotions welled up again and tears fell so hard she couldn't see the computer screen. "Wh-who am I trying to fool? Practically my whole life—with the exception of those eight gaping years—Garrett's been my one constant. He makes me laugh and he holds me when I cry. For the second time his baby's growing inside me and I want to shout it from the rooftops, but I'm afraid. What if I lose this baby? Worse, what if I have a healthy, gorgeous boy or girl only to discover the last thing Garrett wants is to be a father? What then? Because I would never want a man simply because he feels trapped by honor to 'do the right thing' by me." Eve dropped her forehead to her desk. This was all too much.

"Okay, before you whip yourself into additional angst, let's break this down. You mentioned you got the feeling Garrett was relieved you weren't pregnant." Handing Eve a tissue, Darcie pressed, "Could you have misread his reaction? What if instead of him being happy you weren't pregnant, he was actually sad?"

Eve took a moment to mull that over. "I suppose it

could be possible. I mean, every signal he sends makes me think he feels at least a little something for me. Why didn't I just tell him everything—not just about the baby, but how much he's come to mean to me?"

"Know what I think?" Darcie tucked strands of Eve's riotous hair behind her ear. "Maybe Garrett's just as scared as you."

"So what do I do?"

"Easy." Darcie grinned. "March that cute behind of yours to his base and tell him you not only have fallen for him, but you're carrying his future child."

"Yo, Woof!"

On a blustery late-January Friday, Garrett looked up from spraying salt water from his dive gear to see Tristan running toward him. "What's up? You never run unless you're in trouble."

His longtime pal laughed. "Oh, someone's in trouble, all right, but this time it's not me. Chief just got word you've got company up at the gate—*female* company."

"My mom? She okay?"

Tristan took the hose from him, picking up where Garrett had left off. His shoulder was nearly healed. "Think a whole lot younger and named Eve Barnesworth."

"Damn…" Garrett's stomach sank. He'd said all he could that night back in Coral Ridge. What had possessed her to come all the way up here?

"No kidding." Tristan laughed. "Hurry up and see her, so you can bring me details."

"Anyone ever told you, you're worse than a gossipy old woman when it comes to butting into other folks' business?"

His buddy just cast him a supersize cheesy grin.

Even on a borrowed golf cart, it took Garrett a good fifteen minutes to wind his way up to the gate, and once there, the gate guard directed him to a black rental sedan parked in the visitor lot.

Eve appeared to be sleeping.

When he approached, she woke with a start, then exited the car. "Garrett!" she called with a wave.

Lord help him, but his pulse quickened at the sight of her. She was lovely as ever, but dangerous. He wanted her—needed her—too bad, which left him vulnerable to her hurting him all over again. Every soldier knew to never show your enemy your weakness. Eve had hurt him more than a gunshot ever could. He refused to go through that kind of pain again.

"This is a nice surprise." He tried striking a casual tone, as if the act of her being in one of the places he most loved and felt alive hadn't just made his whole year.

"Sorry to barge in like this, I…" Her flighty hands landed in her hair, where the ocean breeze had swept it into her eyes. She wore all white and the color emphasized her fragile, ethereal air and his unquenchable desire to always protect her. "I have something I should've told you back in Coral Ridge, but chickened out."

"O-okay." He braced his left hand on the hood of her car. Whatever she had to say, he wasn't entirely sure he wanted to hear. "Shoot."

She licked her lips. "I was hoping for a more formal setting, but I suppose this will do." A seagull squawked, landing not ten feet away, feasting on bread crusts from someone's lunch.

"I'd offer to at least take you to coffee, but I'm still on duty till five."

"That's okay." Her smile wavered, resulting in him feeling like the world's biggest jackass. "This won't take long."

"Want to at least sit in the car? Get out of the wind?"

"No," she said with a firm shake of her head. "I've kept this from you for a while now—too long—so I might as well just come right out and say it. Remember the night you left when I asked if you'd stay if I was pregnant?"

"Yeah…" His stomach tightened.

"I lied."

"Then, you really…"

She nodded. "Almost ten weeks."

"So then the first time we…"

"I knew right away." She looked to him with her expression hopeful, but Garrett was too rattled to form a sentence. Part of him was elated. A larger part—terrified. He'd been down the exact road with her once before and it'd ended horribly for both. "Aren't you going to say something?"

"Honestly…" He sharply exhaled, then couldn't seem to catch his next breath. "I'm, ah, not sure what to say."

"Then I'll talk. You listen. I can't begin to tell you how sorry I am for keeping this from you, but with the miscarriages I've had and losing Boyd, I was afraid this baby was a dream that might never come true." Hands curved to her belly much the same way the night he'd noticed her doing by the pool, tears welled in her eyes, but she held her emotions in check. "Now that I'm further along than I was with the babies I lost, I'm hopeful—excited, even—for what the future, our *shared* future, may hold. This time, we could go through my pregnancy together. I want you to experience feeling our baby move. And I don't want to go through another labor alone. I'm not afraid to admit I need you, just like I did with our first son, but I was so scared of shaming my father, that in hindsight I failed doing what was the most important thing in the world—calling you."

Hearing this long-awaited confession from her should've made his spirits soar, but Garrett only found himself all the more confused. Removing a notepad from his chest pocket, he jotted down his address. "Do me a favor and meet me here. Say five-thirty?"

"Garrett?" Her raspy tone ripped at his conscience. *She's carrying your baby, man. Seriously? That's all you have to say?* "Would you rather I just leave? Go back to Coral Ridge?"

Part of him wanted badly to grab her up in his arms and never let go. To give her the happy ending she'd obviously chased him down to find. But he just didn't have it in him. He'd stood unflinching with a rifle aimed between his eyes and felt less pressure.

"Garrett, please, say something."

Nodding, shaking his head, he managed to say, "Know this—when the time comes, I will always be there for my child. As for us, yeah, it'd probably be best if you go."

"B-back to Florida?" As long as he lived, he'd carry her pained expression.

"Yes. Please, just go." *Before you destroy me again.*

Chapter Fifteen

"Back up the truck." Because of the gravity of Garrett's situation, Deacon had joined him and Tristan for a night out at Tipsea's, their favorite bar. "She told you she's pregnant and you sent her on her way? Are you nuts? Or really just that big of an ass?"

"Hey, whoa, slow down with the name-calling." Tristan cracked a peanut. "Garrett's been to this rodeo twice with the same gal. Who's to say she's not going to pull the same disappearing stunt all over again?"

"She was sixteen!" Deacon argued, slamming his longneck beer to the counter. "Now, Eve's a grown woman. I seriously doubt she's going to check herself into a home for unwed mothers."

"You don't know what she's liable to do," Tristan countered after his third shot of Jack. "I'm telling you, women are the devil. Nothing but trouble in heels."

Deacon rolled his eyes. "That's whiskey and heartache talking. If Garrett would just—"

Garrett whistled the two of them quiet—no easy feat above blaring honky-tonk and an already rowdy crowd. "How about I get a say in my own affairs?"

"Too late." Deacon signaled the bartender for another

round. "You already blew it. Leave it to us to figure out a way to get Eve to take you back."

Garrett argued, "What if I don't want her?"

"If that were true, you wouldn't have passed on the last five hotties who hit on you."

"EVE, ARE YOU CRAZY?" Dina hustled her in from a frigid downpour. "Get in here before you catch your death of cold."

"S-sorry," Eve said through chattering teeth. "Juanita's in Miami and I—I went to Garrett and told him about the baby, but he told me to go home, but without my dad that giant house doesn't feel like home anymore, and I didn't kn-know where else to go."

"Sweetie…" Dina fussed with taking Eve's trench coat, hanging it on the entry-hall rack, then getting a towel for her hair. "I'm so glad you're here. I was just making a cocoa. Want one?"

"Yes, please."

A fire crackled in the hearth and an old black-and-white movie had been muted on TV. Fat Albert purred on Garrett's father's recliner.

Dina tossed Eve an afghan throw. "Wrap yourself in that and then follow me. Sounds like this situation calls for some good old-fashioned girl talk."

"I'm sorry, I shouldn't have even come." Five minutes later, warm, dry and back in her right mind, Eve realized how crazy she must look to Garrett's mother. "I returned from my flight and it was raining so hard and the house was cold and dark, I needed to be with someone I knew."

"Aw." Dina patted her hand. "I'm flattered you picked me. Wanna know a secret?"

"Sure." Eve's pulse kicked up a notch at whatever Garrett's mom had to tell her. Hopefully she held a happy secret and not anything that would only make her more upset.

"Remember after your father's funeral? And Garrett brought you here?"

"Yes…" Eve remembered all too well how painful that time had been.

"Well, when you woke from your nap and we were in the garden, and I told you us Solomons keep what's ours, I meant it—especially about you."

"Me?" Eyes wide, Eve put her hand to her chest.

"Since you two started grade school, Garrett's always held a soft spot for you. In high school, I secretly hoped you two might one day marry. When you left, it hurt me, too. Something about you has always brought an extra sparkle to my son's eyes. I saw it back when you were kids and it's there again every time he sees you now."

Eve sadly laughed. "That may be but, Dina, I poured my heart out to Garrett. Told him about the baby and he sent me away like I was a stranger. I've never known him to be so cruel."

"Know what I think?" Dina asked while adding cocoa and sugar to a saucepan filled with milk.

Eve was afraid to ask.

"My boy is scared out of his mind that he's going to fall for you all over again and you'll leave him."

"What?" Face pinched, Eve shook her head. "That's ridiculous. Where would I go?"

"That's my point—not that you'll physically leave like you did last time you carried his baby, but you'd leave him behind just the same."

"WITH DR. LOVE PASSED OUT cold," Deacon said on his way into his old apartment living room, "I'm glad we'll finally be able to have a real talk."

"Honestly—" Garrett picked up the remote, surfing through channels for a decent action flick "—I'm over it. Making the decision to be without Eve hurts less than it would to lose her and another kid all over again. Being face-to-face with my son—*my freaking son*—yet not even be able to hug him or tell him I care without coming across like a nut was horrible. I can't imagine going through something like that again. I have to figure out a way to be with my kids, but avoid their mom."

Deacon took the remote and turned off the TV. "Yeah, that seems real smart. Especially when Eve came all this way to pour her heart out to you."

Hand to his forehead, Garrett admitted, "When you put it that way…"

"My point exactly. Our last mission, you babbled about Eve nonstop. Trust me, since I went through something similar with Ellie, I remember the signs. I'm not saying marry Eve tomorrow, but at least give things a chance."

"What about the distance? What if she wants me to give up the navy?"

Deacon held up his hands in surrender. "That, you'll have to take up with Eve and the CO. But if she feels half as much for you as you seem to for her, I'm pretty sure you two will figure it out."

GARRETT DROVE ALL NIGHT.

Only when he got to Eve's mausoleum, he was informed by her security she wasn't home.

Beyond exhausted and feeling darker by the minute

about what he'd done to Eve—what he'd done to his own future should she not forgive him, Garrett headed for his mom's. He'd get a couple hours' sleep then have a better perspective on how to play this out. All he had to do was get Eve to give him another chance and then together, just like Deacon said, they could work out everything else.

He pulled up to his childhood home only to get a shock.

Eve's Jag was parked at the curb.

At five in the morning, he opened the door on a dead-quiet house. He found his mom asleep in her room and Eve crashed in the guest room usually reserved for his aunt Carol. *His* cat was sprawled out on her bed. What was going on? Since when were Eve and his mom pals? Especially when Eve had kept her as much in the dark about her pregnancy as him.

Or had she?

How did you and Eve end things?

She didn't have anything special to tell you?

Holy hell… Had his mom known all along? Kept him as much in the dark as Eve had about his own baby?

Garrett dumped his bag in the middle of the living-room floor, then walked right back out the front door. He needed space to think. Breathe. This changed everything. If he couldn't even trust his own mom, then who?

Eve woke not sure where she was, then it all came rushing back. Cold, Atlantic wind. Garrett asking her to leave in a brittle voice that'd chilled her to her core.

Though sunlight streamed through lace curtains, all Eve wanted to do was pull the covers over her head and hide. Apparently Fat Albert agreed, as he'd stretched across the bed's bottom half and showed no intention of moving. His purring was loud enough to echo.

It was Saturday, so at least she didn't have to worry about facing Darcie at the office. Why hadn't she gone to her last night? Why had she run to Dina for consoling when this time, it'd been her son causing pain?

A knock sounded on the door. "You two all right in there? I'm hoping you have exciting news."

Confused, not even remembering having closed the door, Eve called, "Dina, come in. It's just me."

The door creaked open. Dina gave the room a quick look-see. "How odd…"

With a half laugh, Eve asked, "Who were you expecting?"

"Garrett's ditty bag is in the living room, but he's not here and neither is his car."

Eve's mind raced. "What does that mean?"

"Wish I knew…"

Eve fingered her quilt's lace trim.

Dina asked, "Where do you think he could be?"

With sudden clarity, Eve knew exactly where Garrett would've gone upon finding her at his mother's home. "I have a hunch where to find him."

Out of bed, she took her jeans from where she'd folded them over the footboard, wriggling them up bare legs, not caring if in the process, Dina was given a view. "Got a sweatshirt I can borrow?"

"I have just the thing…"

"THOUGHT I MIGHT FIND you here."

Garrett woke from a fitful sleep to see Eve striding toward him, wearing one of his old Coral Ridge football hoodies. From a distance, softened by morning sun, time had stood still. She was sneaking off from cheer practice for a romantic rendezvous. Here, sheltered by this place time had forgotten, they'd take turns discovering each other, sharing not only their bodies, but minds and hearts.

That was then, but her current betrayal was now. Sitting upright, he said, "You told my mom about the baby, but not me?"

"Not by choice. After I fainted, after you'd gone off to God only knows where, I went to the doctor. Your mom had an appointment that same morning, saw some pregnancy-nutrition brochures I carried and voilà—a classic case of small-town news traveling fast. I assured your mom I would tell you in my own time. Once I was sure I'd carry the baby to term."

"But you're nowhere near a fail-safe date."

"Tell me about it." She cupped her hands to her still-flat belly. "Which is why I've been falling apart on you. More than anything, Garrett, I want this baby. And I want you. I'm sorry if I've yet again hurt you, but you have to know you've hurt me, too. Do you have any idea how bad it stung when you sent me away from your base? I'd traveled all that way to offer my heart to you and you threw my love away."

"Wait— Your love? You love me?"

She threw her hands in the air only to let them slap against her thighs. "Of course I love you. I've always loved you. A thousand of my first marriages couldn't equal a single night spent with you. You make me laugh and hold me when I cry. Your face is the first thing I want to see when I wake in the morning and the last thing I want to see before going to bed at night."

"Eve…" He went to her, hugging her, kissing her,

nuzzling what he knew to be the most sensitive spot on her neck. "I've been such a jerk. Fighting and fighting what I felt for you, all because I was afraid of losing you all over again. I've been so afraid to trust what we share is real, that I've overanalyzed everything. Picking your every word apart."

"It's okay…" She kissed his mouth, his cheeks, his closed eyes. "I love you."

"I love you." He took her by her hands, leading her to the spot on the marble balustrade alongside the cypress where they'd painstakingly carved their initials. "And do you realize the first time we told each other those words was in this same spot?"

She kissed him all over again, he assumed for remembering.

How much time had he wasted with his doubts?

Falling to his knees, he raised the sweatshirt she wore, her T-shirt, kissing her belly and the baby within. "You've made me so happy."

Hands in his hair, she hugged him to her. "Oh, before we get too carried away, which, if you keep nuzzling lower is going to happen in about three minutes, what would you think about us maybe getting a house in Virginia Beach? I'll let Darcie and Zack take over most of Barnesworth's day-to-day operations. The rest I can handle by email, fax and phone."

Glancing up, he froze. "You sure? That's a huge step for you. Barnesworth Industries is your life."

"Correction—*was* my life. Now I have you. And once our baby comes, I want nothing more than to be a full-time mom."

"Woman," Garrett said with a sexy growl, "you keep this up, you're going to kill me with happiness."

"Then I'd better stop."

"Nah…" He unbuttoned her jeans and kept right on kissing.

Epilogue

"Push," Dina urged Eve.

Though Eve had been in hard labor only a few hours, it felt more like a week—especially with her supposed rock, Garrett, looking pastier with each contraction.

"Garrett," Dina snapped, "what's wrong with you? You're a SEAL! How is it you're queasy during the most natural act in the world?"

"Who says I'm queasy?"

Eve glanced toward her man to find him deathly pale and leaning hard to the right.

"I—I'm not believing th-this…" she huffed between rolling bouts of pain. "I—I'm doing all the work. A-all you're supposed to do is h-hold my hand."

He stood, only to wobble. "I'm good."

"S-sit back down," she told him. Delivering their child was proving tough enough without added worry about him. Honestly, the man had been shot. How was he now on the verge of passing out over the birth of their baby girl?

"Nope," he said by her side, "I've got this."

Judging by his still-white complexion, he wasn't even remotely in control, but as her pain increased, thankfully so did his kindness. By the time their daughter entered the world, he'd almost regained his full color.

After finally holding the dear, little infant she'd feared might never come, Eve succumbed to exhaustion. When she woke, she had to pinch herself to make sure she wasn't dreaming. Silhouetted by the rising sun, Garrett held their daughter, Marianne—Mari, for short—named after her mother. The sight of Eve's big, strong man holding their itty-bitty baby girl was too much. Tears fell, but they were happy tears. A sign of deep-felt gratitude for her multitude of blessings.

"Hey, sleeping beauty," Garrett said, warming her through and through with his smile. "Mom went home to get some z's a while ago, but me and Mari were beginning to wonder if you were ever waking up."

"I'm getting around to it." Eve held out her arms. "Bring me that adorable baby."

"Only been married three months and already you're bossing me around."

"Get used to it," she teased before inspecting their baby's perfect fingers and toes.

He kissed her forehead. "Already am."

"I'm almost afraid to ask, but have you heard anything from the Henrys?" Dawn and Steve told Boyd he was their son right before Eve and Garrett's small wedding. The Henrys had brought him to the ceremony and though initial meetings had been awkward, their relationship was moving in the right direction.

"I did, and Dawn promised to bring Boyd by before school."

She winced. "She should've waited until after. That's too long a drive before his classes."

"Would you hush and enjoy the fact that our son

specifically asked to see you, me and the baby *before* school."

"He did?" Eve's heart felt impossibly full.

Garrett nodded, kneeling alongside her and their sleeping daughter.

"Is this really happening?" She cupped his dear cheek. "We're about to have both of our children in the same room?"

"Yep." He leaned in for a kiss. "Crazy, but true."

"I love you," she said with a happy sigh.

"Even though I damn near fainted while you gave birth?"

"*Especially* because of that. You're far too perfect. It's good seeing at least a small chink in your armor."

He tilted his head back and groaned. "Why do I have the feeling I'm never going to live that down?"

"Because you're not?" Grinning, she tugged him in for a kiss.

A knock sounded on the hospital-room door, then Dawn, Steve and Boyd came into the room.

"She's so tiny…" Boyd said from beside the bed, his eyes wide with wonder. "Was I that small?" he asked Dawn.

"Yes, you were." His adopted mother stood behind him, wrapping him in a hug. There had been a time when Eve had been jealous of Dawn's closeness to her son, but she now appreciated the woman's love. Dawn and Steve had given Boyd the stability Eve wasn't sure she and Garrett would've been able to provide—at least not back when he'd been born.

In a couple weeks, the renovations on the beach house they'd purchased in Virginia Beach would be finished and stability would be Eve's new middle name.

Dina would have her own private guesthouse, so when Garrett was deployed, the women in his life would have each other for company.

Boyd said, "She kinda looks like me."

"She sure does." Garrett stood alongside their son. "But I bet she won't be able to kick a soccer ball near as hard as you."

"Hey!" Eve and Dawn said laughingly at the same time.

"This little girl will be able to do anything she sets her mind to." Eve traced her baby's nose.

"Agreed," Dawn said. To Boyd, she asked, "Ready to get to school?"

"I guess. But will we get to see Mari again? And where's Grandma Dina? Thought she was gonna be here?"

"Of course you'll see Mari." Garrett ruffled the boy's hair. "She's your sister. And my mom said she'll see you at your school play on Friday night."

"Oh, yeah." Boyd smiled, completing Eve's perfect new world. "I forgot. You and Eve are coming, too, right?"

"Absolutely," Eve said with a quick smile.

Boyd hugged Garrett, then Eve, and even Mari. "I'm going to be a real good big brother."

"Cool." Garrett must've noticed the size of their son's grin, too, as he took Eve's hand, giving her a discreet squeeze.

Once their visitors had gone, Garrett climbed into the bed alongside her. "Happy?"

"Beyond." With their daughter nestled between them, they shared a kiss. "Did you ever dream we'd have both a son and daughter in this short a time?"

"Honestly?" he said with a chuckle. "No. But I've gotta say, if being a parent is this much fun, how about we start right away on more?"

"Absolutely, but under one condition."

"What's that?" He kissed her again—this time, thoroughly enough for her to feel his love all the way to her toes.

"You're going to have to man up during delivery. If any of your big, strong SEAL friends knew the kind of wuss they've been working with, they'd laugh you out of the navy."

"You're killing me," he said with a laugh, "but all right, you have a deal."

* * * * *

Be sure to look for THE SEAL'S VALENTINE,
the next book in Laura Marie Altom's
OPERATION: FAMILY series!
Available in January 2013!

COMING NEXT MONTH
from Harlequin® American Romance®

AVAILABLE JANUARY 2, 2013

#1433 A CALLAHAN OUTLAW'S TWINS
Callahan Cowboys
Tina Leonard

When Kendall Phillips announces she is pregnant with Sloan Callahan's twin sons, the loner ex-military man realizes he has to change his outlaw ways...and start thinking of a way to propose!

#1434 REMEMBER ME, COWBOY
Coffee Creek, Montana
C.J. Carmichael

An accident left Corb Lambert with amnesia and he can't remember Laurel Sheridan, let alone getting her pregnant. Will a hasty marriage solve these problems—or make them worse?

#1435 THE SEAL'S VALENTINE
Operation: Family
Laura Marie Altom

Navy SEAL Tristan Bartoni's heart was broken when his wife left him and took their son. So how can he be attracted to Brynn Langtoine and risk his heart again for her and her cute kids?

#1436 HER RANCHER HERO
Saddlers Prairie
Ann Roth

Cody Naylor fosters four troubled boys on Hope Ranch. Is it appropriate that Cody is falling for his new housekeeper? Will her leaving at the end of the summer throw the boys into turmoil? Or just Cody?

REQUEST YOUR FREE BOOKS!
2 FREE NOVELS PLUS 2 FREE GIFTS!

LOVE, HOME & HAPPINESS

YES! Please send me 2 FREE Harlequin® American Romance® novels and my 2 FREE gifts (gifts are worth about $10). After receiving them, if I don't wish to receive any more books, I can return the shipping statement marked "cancel." If I don't cancel, I will receive 4 brand-new novels every month and be billed just $4.49 per book in the U.S. or $5.24 per book in Canada. That's a saving of at least 14% off the cover price! It's quite a bargain! Shipping and handling is just 50¢ per book in the U.S. and 75¢ per book in Canada.* I understand that accepting the 2 free books and gifts places me under no obligation to buy anything. I can always return a shipment and cancel at any time. Even if I never buy another book, the two free books and gifts are mine to keep forever.

154/354 HDN FEP2

Name _____ (PLEASE PRINT)

Address _____ Apt. #

City _____ State/Prov. _____ Zip/Postal Code

Signature (if under 18, a parent or guardian must sign)

Mail to the **Reader Service:**
IN U.S.A.: P.O. Box 1867, Buffalo, NY 14240-1867
IN CANADA: P.O. Box 609, Fort Erie, Ontario L2A 5X3

Not valid for current subscribers to Harlequin American Romance books.

Want to try two free books from another line?
Call 1-800-873-8635 or visit www.ReaderService.com.

* Terms and prices subject to change without notice. Prices do not include applicable taxes. Sales tax applicable in N.Y. Canadian residents will be charged applicable taxes. Offer not valid in Quebec. This offer is limited to one order per household. All orders subject to credit approval. Credit or debit balances in a customer's account(s) may be offset by any other outstanding balance owed by or to the customer. Please allow 4 to 6 weeks for delivery. Offer available while quantities last.

Your Privacy—The Reader Service is committed to protecting your privacy. Our Privacy Policy is available online at www.ReaderService.com or upon request from the Reader Service.

We make a portion of our mailing list available to reputable third parties that offer products we believe may interest you. If you prefer that we not exchange your name with third parties, or if you wish to clarify or modify your communication preferences, please visit us at www.ReaderService.com/consumerschoice or write to us at Reader Service Preference Service, P.O. Box 9062, Buffalo, NY 14269. Include your complete name and address.

HAR11B

Turn the page for a preview of

THE OTHER SIDE OF US

by

Sarah Mayberry,

*coming January 2013
from Harlequin® Superromance®.*

*PLUS, exciting changes are in the works!
Enjoy the same great stories in a longer format
and new look—beginning January 2013!*

THE OTHER SIDE OF US
A brand-new novel
from Harlequin® Superromance® author
Sarah Mayberry

In recovery from a serious accident, Mackenzie Williams
is beating all the doctors' predictions. But she needs
single-minded focus. She doesn't *need the distraction*
of neighbors—especially good-looking ones
like Oliver Garrett!

MACKENZIE BREATHED DEEPLY to recover from the workout. She'd pushed herself too far but she wanted to accelerate her rehabilitation. Still, she needed to lie down to combat the nausea and shaking muscles.

There was a knock on the front door. Who on earth would be visiting her on a Thursday morning? Probably a cold-calling salesperson.

She answered, but her pithy rejection died before she'd formed the first words.

The man on her doorstep was definitely not a cold caller. Nothing about this man was cold, from the auburn of his wavy hair to his brown eyes to his sensual mouth. Nothing cold about those broad shoulders, flat belly and lean hips, either.

"Hey," he said in a shiver-inducing baritone. "I'm Oliver Garrett. I moved in next door." His smile was so warm and vibrant it was almost offensive.

"Mackenzie Williams." Oh, no. Her legs were starting to

tremble, indicating they wouldn't hold up long. Any second now she would embarrass herself in front of this complete and very good-looking stranger.

"It's been years since I was down here." He seemed to settle in for a chat. "It doesn't look as though—"

"I have to go." Her stomach rolled as she shut the door. The last thing she registered was the look of shock on Oliver's face at her abrupt dismissal.

And somehow she knew their neighborly relations would be a lot cooler now.

Will Mackenzie be able to make it up to Oliver for her rude introduction? Find out in THE OTHER SIDE OF US by Sarah Mayberry, available January 2013 from Harlequin® Superromance®. PLUS, exciting changes are in the works! Enjoy the same great stories in a longer format and new look—beginning January 2013!

It all starts with a kiss

Check out the brand-new series

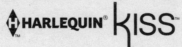

Fun, flirty and sensual romances.
ON SALE JANUARY 22!